About the author

David Fuller is an FA-qualifie
currently coaches a youth footl
He has worked as a journalist for more than a decade,
during which time he has written for numerous
publications on a variety of different subjects. David
lives in Newhaven, East Sussex with his wife, two
sons and cat Merry.

Other books by David Fuller

Alfie Jones and a change of fortune
Alfie Jones and a test of character
Alfie Jones and the missing link
Alfie Jones and an uncertain future

To Sophia James

RDF Publishing

3 Courtlands Mews, Church Hill, Newhaven,
East Sussex,
BN9 9LU

Alfie Jones and the big decision
A RDF Publishing book

First published in Great Britain by RDF Publishing in 2015
Printed and bound in Great Britain by Clays Ltd,
St Ives plc.

1

Text copyright © David Fuller
Images courtesy of Rob Smyth
(www.robsmythart.com)

David Fuller asserts the moral right to
be identified as the author of this work

ISBN 978-0-9570339-4-8

For more exclusive Alfie Jones content, visit:
www.alfie-jones.co.uk

ALFIE JONES AND THE BIG DECISION

DAVID FULLER

Illustrated by
Rob Smyth

www.alfie-jones.co.uk

Prologue

It hadn't taken long for the small, blond curly haired boy to catch the watching scout's eye.

With only ten minutes of the match gone, the left midfielder had already been heavily involved in the game.

One moment he had denied an opponent a clear goal scoring opportunity after making a sublime sliding tackle. The next he had come close to scoring himself, with a superbly struck angled drive which had missed the intended target by mere inches.

As the half wore on, the scout hadn't been able to stop himself from nodding appreciatively over and over again at the performance being put in by the blue team's number 11. He was only too aware that if anyone had been paying him any attention, he would have undoubtedly resembled one of those nodding dogs that you sometimes see in the back of people's cars.

Fortunately, though, all the eyes of the various adults and children in attendance were glued to the action on the pitch, rather than on him.

The scout plunged his hand into one of his coat pockets, searching for his notebook and pencil so that he could make a note of the young boy's name.

It was only when he was unable to find what he'd been looking for that he remembered he wasn't actually supposed to be working. He had only popped out to buy a Sunday paper for his parents, with whom he was staying for the weekend.

Having decided to take a shortcut through the recreation ground, he'd noticed that a game of football was just about to start, so had decided to stay and watch for a while.

He was glad that he had.

As the blond haired boy played yet another simple but effective pass, the scout decided that, working or not, it was time to find out the young boy's name.

This was a player who needed – and deserved – to be watched again.

He'd just begun strolling towards the man whom he assumed to be the blue team's coach, intending to ask him for the number 11's name, when that particular query was answered for him.

Three youngsters who were watching the game from the sideline all started loudly chanting a player's name. It was clear from the way the small curly-haired boy looked at them and then blushed that they were singing about him.

Question answered.

It was a name the scout was sure would be easy enough to remember.

The man glanced at his watch. He'd already been gone for over half-an-hour. The trip to the newsagents shouldn't have taken him any more than ten minutes maximum.

Resolving that he really ought to get going and realising that it must be almost half-time, the scout turned to leave when, somewhat against the run of play, the team in the red and white striped shirts took the lead.

'Let's just see how the number 11 reacts to the disappointment of his team going a goal behind,' he mused silently. 'All good players need to show spirit, no matter what the score.'

Within seconds the scout had his answer.

Following a positive run forward by the only girl playing in the match, the ball deflected in the direction of the number 11. Even though two opposition players were closer to the ball than he was, the left midfielder managed to reach it first.

His first touch was perfect. He looked up at the goal. He glanced quickly at the ball. He set his sights.

With one smooth movement he curled a delightful left footed shot into the top corner of the goal. It was an impeccable finish and the ideal response to going a goal behind.

Now the scout was torn. He knew he really should be getting back to his parent's house with their newspapers, but he just couldn't bring himself to stop watching this young boy in action. Determination, speed, skill, a good range of passing and impressive shooting ability... this youngster seemed to have it all.

As the referee blew the whistle for half-time, the scout darted off to the paper shop. His plan was to go and buy the papers now, and then get back in time to watch a bit of the second half, just to see if he could add stamina to his ever growing mental list of the boy's talents.

The second half was just getting underway by the time he arrived breathlessly back at the pitch.

The red and white team started the second half strongly, completely dominating the match. In fact, aside from the number 11, who was simply everywhere, most of the other blue team players appeared to have lost interest.

After just a few minutes of the second half, the man finally decided to tear himself away from the game and return to his parent's house.

It wasn't a lack of interest that ultimately influenced his decision to leave. Nor was it the guilt at having spent far longer than intended – and needed – in collecting the newspapers.

Instead it was the rather bizarre behaviour of one of the watching boys, who could easily have passed as a man such was his sheer size, which finally persuaded the scout to head home.

Since the start of the second half, the young spectator had been continually jigging up and down on the spot, singing songs that seemed to bear no relation to the game going on in front of him. As the odd child's singing grew louder and louder, and increasingly annoying, the scout decided that he simply couldn't stand it any longer and so turned and left.

He'd already seen enough to know that it would not be the last time he would watch the blue team's number 11 in action, though.

Chapter one

Six months later

As Alfie Jones walked briskly towards the notice board outside the boy's changing room, his heart skipped a beat. From across the corridor he had noticed that a piece of paper had finally been pinned to the previously empty space located below the 'Year 7 Boys Football' header.

It had been over a week since Tideway Secondary School had held its first and only trial for the Year 7 football teams and Alfie had been starting to wonder whether the 'A' and 'B' squads for the first school matches of the season would ever be announced.

Subconsciously, Alfie crossed his fingers

as he stared anxiously up at the squad
lists, desperately hoping to see his
name included under the column clearly
marked 'A-Team' in dark red ink.

He wasn't to be disappointed.

It took all of Alfie's will power to stop
himself from screaming excitedly at the
top of his voice, such was his utter delight
at seeing his name included as part of the
A-Team squad.

Studying the list a little closer, he
wasn't at all surprised to note that his
close friends Billy Morris and Hayden
Whitlock had also been selected for
the school's top team. They were both
members of professional club Kingsway

United's Under 12s Academy, after all.

More of a shock, though, was that Liam Walker was only included in the B-Team squad.

Like Alfie, Liam played for the Kingsway Colts Under 12s and was also a member of the Kingsway United Elite Centre. Although he may not have been the most technically gifted player, one thing Liam certainly knew how to do was score goals. He'd been the Colts' leading scorer every season since the under 9s, and had already scored 10 goals from the team's first five matches of the current campaign.

Alfie knew that his friend would be devastated not to have made the school's main team. But, if truth be told, he was feeling so elated right at that moment, that nothing could have darkened his mood.

It took Alfie a few seconds longer to realise that he was, in fact, the only Colts player to have been selected for the school's A-Team. Secretly, this discovery only served to enhance his already buoyant mood – not that he would ever admit this to anyone else, of course.

So intently was he staring at the notice board, at least at the section where his name was written, that Alfie hadn't realised that someone had been standing beside him for a good 30 seconds, trying to attract his attention.

"Earth to Alfie, come in Alfie Jones," he eventually heard a familiar voice say.

"Oh... hi Billy," he replied. "Sorry about that. I was miles away."

"I could tell." Billy laughed good-naturedly. The two boys had been best friends for years, and although they didn't see so much of each other now that they were in different classes and Billy no longer played for the Colts, they still enjoyed little more than spending time together. "I see congratulations are in order," Billy added, nodding his head in the direction of the notice board.

"Yeah. I can't believe I got in if I'm being honest. It'll be great getting the chance to play alongside you and Hayden again," Alfie enthused.

"You deserve it, Alf. You were awesome in the trial. Keep playing like that and you're bound to get a chance to try out for the United Academy soon."

"Yeah... maybe... hopefully," Alfie responded, a mixture of disappointment and frustration in his voice.

Overall, things had been going well for

Alfie in recent months. Having just about managed to keep the Colts together at the end of the previous season, the team had started the current season on fire. They had won all of their first five games and Alfie had been an integral part of the team's impressive start.

While it may have been Liam who was grabbing most of the goals, it was without a doubt Alfie who had become the team's star player.

He'd also settled well into his new school. He had been extremely nervous about starting secondary school, especially once he'd discovered that he was not going to be in the same class as Billy, Hayden or Liam. However, Alfie had soon made new friends and quickly realised that all the horror stories he'd previously heard about Year 7 boys having their heads flushed down the toilet by the older children were simply not true.

Being picked for the school's top football team had only served to round off a promising first month at Tideway Secondary School.

Yet if there was one major complaint that the young boy had with his life at the moment, it was the fact that he still hadn't been offered a trial at the Kingsway United – or indeed any other – Academy.

A few years earlier, Alfie had been told by a mysterious fortune teller called Madam Zola that he would one day become a professional footballer, just so long as he listened to and acted appropriately on any advice she gave him.

Over the past few years, the fortune teller had repeatedly assured him that he was still on course to fulfil his destiny. Yet the more time passed without him being offered even a trial for a professional club's academy, the more Alfie found himself seriously starting to doubt whether Madam Zola's prediction would ever come true.

He'd once read in his favourite football magazine, *Kick Off*, that the vast majority of professional footballers were in a pro-team's academy by the time they were 12. Alfie had turned 12 just under two weeks ago and couldn't help but think that something needed to happen sooner rather than later.

Still, he knew that what Billy had just said was right; the only way he could hope to get a trial was to continue to play well and work hard at improving his all-round game.

"I shouldn't think Liam will be too happy about not being in the A-Team," Billy stated, having had the chance to properly study the squad lists himself. "Actually, we should get going. I don't want to be here when he comes to check and realises that he's not with us in the A-Team. You know how sulky he can be!"

Alfie nodded his agreement and was just about to follow his friend back down the corridor when he realised something else. Something that made him grin from ear-to-ear.

"Jasper's not in either squad," he said, not even attempting to hide the delight in his voice.

For some years, Jasper Johnson had been Alfie's one and only nemesis – well, aside from his younger sister Megan, that is.

Their rivalry stretched back to when Jasper's Dad, Keith, had for a short while been the Kingsway Colts' coach when they were in the under 9s. Both father and son had made those few weeks a wretched time for Alfie; so much so that he had come close to quitting the Colts.

The hostility between the two –

especially on Jasper's part – had not diminished over the years.

"Awesome," Billy declared. "Now come on, hurry up. I can see Liam walking this way."

Alfie and Billy hurried down the corridor in the opposite direction, before Liam could notice them. "I wonder how badly he'll take the news?" Billy asked.

They had barely reached the end of the corridor, when they heard a voice loudly and angrily exclaim: "The B Team? No way! That is an absolute joke. Outrageous."

The two friends looked at each other and smiled. "I guess that answers your question," Alfie chuckled.

Chapter two

By the time the bell rang to signal the end of school later that day, Alfie was still buzzing about being picked to play for the A Team.

Over 90 children had attended the Year 7 boys football trials eight days earlier. Out of all of those he'd been just one of 16 to be selected to participate in the school's first match against Longford Hill Secondary the following Monday. He couldn't help but feel immensely proud of himself.

Alfie had spent the entire afternoon daydreaming about football; even more than usual. He kept imagining how cool it would be to score the Year 7 football team's first ever goal.

He was still lost in thought as he strolled unhurriedly along the corridor towards the exit. So much so that he failed to realise he was being watched until it was too late.

"Yoo-hoo. Alfie," he heard the girl shout.

Alfie uttered a curse under his breath. He instantly knew who was calling him. Daisy Saunders.

Without breaking stride, Alfie put his head down, picked up his pace and strode determinedly towards the door. He desperately hoped that his cheeks weren't glowing bright red. Unfortunately for him, they were.

In the five weeks since he'd started at Tideway Secondary School, barely a day had passed where Daisy hadn't called out his name whenever he happened to walk past her.

While Alfie knew that the girl was a friend of Chloe Reed, who was in turn one of his closest friends, he couldn't remember ever having actually spoken to Daisy before. Therefore, he couldn't understand why she always seemed to be calling and waving to him.

At the start of the week, Alfie had resolved to scour each and every school corridor prior to walking down it, just to make sure that Daisy wasn't nearby. He'd almost made it to the end of Wednesday without being bothered by her, but so consumed was he by thoughts of football on that particular afternoon, that he'd been careless and forgotten to carry out his check.

He would have kicked himself right there and then had he not been so entirely focussed on reaching the door before she could call his name again.

Once outside, Alfie broke into a gentle jog, determined to get as far away from the girl as possible. He didn't really think that she would follow him... but he wasn't going to take any chances. He didn't understand girls at all. Who knew how their minds worked?

Alfie was supposed to be meeting Billy, Hayden and Liam by the school gates so that they could walk home together. Deciding, though, that by waiting he could risk another unwanted meeting with Daisy, he upped his pace and sprinted straight past the gates. His friends had already started teasing him about the girl. There was no way he was going to give them any further excuse to carry on doing so.

As he passed through the gates he could

see that Liam was already there waiting. Luckily, his friend didn't seem to have spotted him, so Alfie kept on running. He ran until he considered himself to be a safe distance away from the school.

He had just slowed back down to walking pace when he felt someone tap him lightly on the shoulder.

Alfie's heart skipped a beat. 'Surely she couldn't have chased me all this way', he thought to himself. 'Could she?'

Slowly, Alfie turned around to face the person who had prodded him. He feared the worst.

"What is wrong with you?" a girl's voice asked once Alfie was facing her. "You look truly petrified."

"Chloe, it's only you. Thank goodness for that." The relief was clearly audible in the young boy's voice.

Up until the beginning of the new football season, Chloe had been one of Alfie's teammates at the Kingsway Colts. Although she had since left the team to join a newly formed girl's football club, the two had remained good friends. In fact, Alfie counted Chloe as his only proper female friend.

"Who did you think it was going to be?" Chloe asked, sounding confused, and a touch concerned. "Is someone after you? It's not Jasper, is it? He's not picking on you again, is he?"

"No, it's nothing like that," Alfie replied. A sheepish look had appeared on his face. "It's... nothing... don't worry about it."

Chloe studied Alfie's face and couldn't fail to notice that her friend was steadily turning a crimson shade of red. "Alfie... does this have something to do with Daisy Saunders?" she asked, unable to hide the amusement from her tone.

Briefly, Alfie considered lying but quickly realised that it would be a waste of time. Somehow, Chloe always seemed to know when he was being truthful and when he wasn't. His mum was able to do the exact same thing. He guessed that it must be a special power that only girls have. One that he just didn't understand.

"She's always bothering me," Alfie blurted out. "I've never even spoken to her, yet whenever I'm near her she shouts out my name. It's really annoying... and embarrassing!"

Chloe laughed loudly.

"What's so funny?" Alfie enquired, sounding more than a tad sorry for himself. "It is really annoying."

"Oh Alfie, you do make me smile,"

Chloe answered, while affectionately ruffling her friend's blond curly hair. "She just thinks you're sweet, that's all. She only calls your name to try and get your attention... and because she knows it embarrasses you and she finds your reaction quite funny."

"She thinks I'm sweet?" Alfie repeated, sounding genuinely surprised.

"Why else do you think she keeps calling you?"

Alfie shrugged his shoulders. "Don't know," he replied honestly. "Never really thought about it."

"Soooo..." Chloe began, raising her eyebrows as a means of encouraging Alfie to continue speaking.

Alfie looked confused. "Soooo... what?"

Chloe sighed frustratedly and rolled her eyes. "So what are you going to do about it?"

The confused expression remained steadfastly on Alfie's face. "About what?"

"On my word, Alfie. Do I really have to spell it out for you?" Chloe was starting to get a little exasperated by Alfie's cluelessness. "Daisy really fancies you. So what are you going to do about it?"

Alfie could feel the heat rushing to his face. "Erm... I... erm... I... Did you see I made the school A Team?" he replied, in a desperate bid to try and change the topic of the conversation.

"Yes I did, Alfie. Well done. Now, about Daisy..."

"It'll be really cool to play in the same team as Billy and Hayden again," Alfie continued, not willing to give Chloe a chance to start babbling about Daisy again. "I'm surprised Liam was only selected for the B Team, though," he quickly added.

Correctly sensing that there would be more chance of getting blood out of a stone than there was of convincing Alfie to say anything more about Daisy, Chloe simply smiled and said: "Have it your way, Alfie. We'll talk about football. But, honestly, so what if Daisy does like you? Is that really such a bad thing?"

The two friends walked on together for a while longer, chatting mostly about football, but also about how much, to both their surprise, they were actually enjoying secondary school.

As they strolled, Alfie couldn't help but think about some of what Chloe had just told him. Was it really such a bad thing if Daisy Saunders did like him? He'd never really contemplated having a proper girlfriend before. Now that he thought about it, though, he supposed that Daisy was quite pretty. 'Maybe I should get to know her better,' he mused. 'Maybe she might like football too... after all, Chloe does,' he reasoned to himself.

Arriving some minutes later outside the newsagents located at the end of the road where Alfie lived, the two friends said goodbye to each other.

Being a Wednesday, the newest edition of Alfie's favourite football magazine, *Kick Off*, would be out and as he did every Wednesday afternoon, he popped inside to buy it.

Alfie would have asked Chloe to wait for him, but he knew that the shop's elderly owner, Sammy Reeve, would no doubt want to talk to him about football. He would be lucky to get out the shop within half-an-hour. Not that he really minded. He liked Sammy a lot. The old man had even once helped Alfie solve a puzzle that had been baffling him for days.

As it turned out, the young boy was only half-right.

He was indeed in the shop for a great deal longer than he really needed to be. It was the reason why he was wrong about.

Chapter three

Alfie should have realised that something was wrong the second he opened the shop's door.

Perhaps, had his head not been so crammed full of thoughts about football and, for the first time in his life, a girl, he would have noticed.

He'd been going to Sammy Reeves' shop for as long as he could remember. Without fail, every time he, or anyone else for that matter, walked into the newsagents, a little bell that was attached to the door would ring to alert Sammy that someone had entered.

On that particular day, had Alfie been paying attention, he would surely have realised that the ring of the bell sounded somewhat different to normal. In fact, it didn't sound like the ring of a bell at all. It sounded more like the tinkling of a wind chime.

Upon entering the shop, the young boy could immediately see that Sammy wasn't sitting on his stool behind the counter. This wasn't particularly unusual. Sammy spent a lot of time in the store room located at the far end of the newsagents. While the old man would insist that he was merely sorting through old newspapers and magazines while he was in there, most of his regular customers thought it was more likely he was napping.

It was because of the amount of time he spent in the store room – either working or sleeping, depending on who you chose to believe – that he had many years ago decided to attach the bell to the door.

Automatically, Alfie ambled over to the magazine shelf, plucked a copy of *Kick Off* from the rack, and then made his way back towards the counter at the front of the shop to pay.

Usually, Sammy would have by now shuffled out of the store room and been making his way ever so slowly towards the till, ready to engage Alfie with some football chatter. Today, though, he was still nowhere to be seen.

'He must be having a really good sleep this afternoon,' the young boy thought to himself, a smile spreading across his face as he pictured the old man snoring contentedly among the discarded newspapers and magazines.

"Sammy," Alfie called out gently, not wanting to startle the old man awake.

Nothing happened.

"Sammy," he repeated, a little louder this time.

Still nothing happened.

Following a few further failed attempts to stir the shopkeeper from his supposed slumber, Alfie began to feel a pang of concern regarding the old man's whereabouts. What if Sammy had slipped and hurt himself? Or worse?

Resolving to go and check on him, Alfie began to venture in the direction of the store room.

It was then that he saw her.

"Hello Alfie," Madam Zola exclaimed cheerfully. The old lady was standing by the magazine rack that Alfie had walked from mere moments earlier. "How are you?" she asked, waving her right hand enthusiastically at him.

For a good few seconds, Alfie stood rooted to the spot, staring dumbfoundedly at the elderly fortune teller. The shock of seeing her had momentarily rendered him physically unable to move.

Then, suddenly remembering what he had been on his way to do, Alfie shook his head and continued on his way towards the store room. "I have to check on Sammy," he said as he marched purposefully towards the back of the shop.

"Sammy's fine, Alfie. He's just popped out to get... erm... something," the fortune teller replied.

Alfie stopped in his tracks and slowly turned to face Madam Zola. "How do you know?" he asked, a hint of suspicion in his tone.

"Because I was in here getting... erm... something, when he suddenly remembered that he needed to get the thing he needed – I forget what it was – and asked me to keep an eye on the shop for him."

The young boy's big blue eyes narrowed as he carefully studied Madam Zola's face.

"How do you know Sammy? How does he know you? I've never heard him

mention you before. Or ever seen you in here for that matter."

"Oh... erm... well... everyone knows Sammy, don't they! I wouldn't say he knows me that well... I suppose I must just have an honest face." Madam Zola smiled and nodded assuredly, as though she was happy with the answer she'd given.

Then, before Alfie could ask her anything further, she quickly added: "Anyway, what's with all these questions? Sammy's fine, that's all you need to worry about. Now, why don't you come over here and talk to me."

The young boy hesitated momentarily.

He couldn't quite understand why Sammy would ask a virtual stranger to look after his shop for him.

At the same time, though, he was delighted to see the fortune teller once again and was equally intrigued to hear what she had to say. There always seemed to be a reason behind his meetings with Madam Zola.

Convincing himself that Sammy would be fine, Alfie walked over to the old lady and gave her an awkward hug.

The fortune teller's face was lit up by a beaming smile and her friendly brown eyes twinkled with sheer delight. "You're getting big," she declared, taking a step back to fully examine her young friend. "It's hard to believe you're the same little boy that strolled into my tent at that fairground nearly three years ago."

For the umpteenth time that day, Alfie could feel his cheeks flush and he knew he'd be starting to redden.

Sensing his unease, and realising she probably sounded an awful lot like one of those elderly, slightly dotty aunts who you only ever see at Christmas, Madam Zola swiftly changed the topic of conversation to one she knew he'd be more comfortable with: Football.

"Well done on getting in the school football team by the way. The A Team, as well. You must be delighted."

That the fortune teller already knew he was in the school football team, without him even having to say anything, came as no surprise to Alfie. She always knew everything there was to know about him.

The two spent the next 20 minutes conversing easily with one another. However, to Alfie's growing frustration, not once did Madam Zola say anything that he deemed to be important with regards to his future.

He then noticed the fortune teller glance down agitatedly at her left wrist, as if she was checking the time.

She never wore a watch, but Alfie knew that whenever Madam Zola started looking at her wrist, she was getting ready to go.

"Madam Zola, is what you told me all those years ago still going to come true?" he asked suddenly, fearing their time together was nearing an end. "Am I still going to become a professional footballer one day?"

Madam Zola smiled warmly at the boy, although she looked a little confused as to why he had asked such a question. "Why, of course, Alfie. Why would you think it wouldn't?"

"It's just that, I'm 12 and I've still not had a trial for a professional team's Academy. I've been at the Kingsway United Elite Centre for over a year now, and been playing really well, I think. Yet they still haven't asked me to try out. Surely it needs to happen soon."

Madam Zola paused for a moment. Alfie could see from the expression on her face that she was carefully considering her response. "The path to our dream is not always the one we would expect to take," she declared eventually.

A frown creased Alfie's face and he scratched the top of his head as he tried to puzzle out what the fortune teller was talking about. Unable to do so, he decided to ask her. He wasn't overly surprised by her response.

"I haven't got time to explain now," she answered hurriedly. "I can't believe I've been in here so long. I only popped in to get... erm... something or another. Now suddenly..." she glanced at her watch-less wrist again, "... it's this time already and I'm still here. I really do need to get going! Bye Alfie." Madam Zola turned and walked briskly to the door.

"But Madam Zola," Alfie yelled after her. "You're supposed to be looking after the shop for..."

However, the fortune teller had flung the door open and stepped outside onto the pavement before he'd even been able to finish his sentence. This time Alfie did hear the sound of a wind chime chiming as the door opened, even though he could see the usual bell still hung from it.

At first, Alfie went to follow her out of the shop. Then, realising that he couldn't leave the newsagents completely unattended, he halted and instead made his way back towards the counter. He hoped Sammy wouldn't be too much longer, wherever it was he'd gone.

The young boy had just settled on the shop keeper's stool to flick through his magazine, when he heard a strange noise coming from the store room.

It sounded like someone groaning. He then heard slow but steady footsteps making their way towards him.

Alfie crouched down behind the counter, his heartbeat racing. He was convinced that there must have been a burglar hiding at the back of the shop the whole time he'd been in there.

Resolving to make a dash for the front

door, Alfie was just about to move when the person fully emerged from the store room.

"Hi-ya, Alfie," yawned Sammy Reeves, stretching both arms high above his head. "Sorry about that, I must have nodded off for a while. It's tiring work sorting through all those old newspapers and magazines, you know."

Alfie rubbed his eyes in disbelief. Sammy had been in the store room all along. Madam Zola had been lying to him.

He quickly stood up and walked over to the shop window, peering desperately up and down the street, but he could see no sign of her. The fortune teller was long gone.

"So," continued Sammy lazily, "what did I miss?"

Chapter four

Fortunately, the still sleepy Sammy Reeves was not in his usual talkative mood.

Therefore, instead of being in the shop for a further half-an-hour, Alfie managed to limit his conversation with the old man to just 15 minutes, without needing to be too abrupt with his responses.

Not once during their briefer than usual chat did Alfie mention Madam Zola. She'd previously warned him never to tell anyone else about her, stating that his destiny would not come true if he did. Angry though he may have been with the fortune teller at that particular moment – he couldn't understand why she had lied to him about Sammy – Alfie would never do anything that could potentially threaten his chance of one day becoming a professional footballer.

Mooching slowly towards his parents' house, the young boy's head was in a whirl as he thought about everything that had happened that day. First he'd been selected for the school football team; then he'd discovered that a girl possibly fancied him; and now he'd just met Madam Zola again.

As was so often the case, Alfie's meeting with the fortune teller had only served to leave him feeling more confused than normal.

'The path to our dream is not always the one we would expect to take.' That's what she'd said to him. But what did it mean? What other possible path could there be? If he couldn't get into a pro-team's academy soon, then surely there was no chance of him ever becoming a professional footballer!

Turning into the road in which he lived, Alfie suddenly realised that he hadn't checked his mobile phone since leaving school. Not even to take it off silent. Usually this was the first thing that he did as soon as the end-of-school bell sounded. He simply couldn't wait to see whether anyone had called or messaged him during the day.

They rarely, if ever, had.

Today, though, a whole host of missed calls and text message notifications were displayed on the screen. They were all from Billy, Hayden and Liam, each of whom was wondering why he hadn't met them after school.

Alfie was still busy texting his friends back when he reached his house a few moments later. He'd decided to tell them that he had been given a detention during his last lesson. He figured this sounded better than telling them the truth; namely that he'd been running away from a girl.

He had only made it halfway up the garden path, when his Mum suddenly burst excitedly from the house to meet him.

"Oh, Alfie, where have you been?" she asked, barely pausing for breath. "Oh, it's Wednesday isn't it? You've no doubt been speaking to old Sammy at the paper shop," she continued, answering her own question. "Come on Alfie, don't dawdle now. I've got something to show you." She rushed back in the direction of the house, almost skipping as she went.

Unfortunately for Mrs Jones, her son was so engrossed with the device in his hand, that he'd barely even registered his Mum was there, let alone noticed that she was so obviously excited about something.

Glancing back over her shoulder, and noticing that Alfie was still sauntering up the path at barely a snail's pace, Mrs Jones quickly decided that a different tact was required.

"Alfie Jones," she said in her sternest sounding voice. "If you don't get here this instant, then I will take that phone off you and you won't see it again until the weekend."

This made Alfie glance up. The fact of the matter was that he hadn't actually heard a word his Mum had just said. However, he could tell from the way she had said it that she was cross about something.

"Oh, hi Mum. Sorry, didn't see you there. Everything okay?"

"Will you just come here please?" the excitable tone had already returned to her voice. "I've got something to show you. I want to know what it is."

"Just give me a minute, Mum," replied Alfie, switching his gaze back down to his phone. "I just need to finish sending this..."

"NOW, Alfie!" Mrs Jones snapped.

Alfie tutted, rolled his eyes, tapped at the screen of his phone to send the message he'd been typing, then placed the device back into his coat pocket and moved (fairly) swiftly into the house.

No sooner was Alfie inside did his Mum come bounding over to him, flapping a white envelope in his direction so enthusiastically that she only just avoided slapping him in the face with it. "You've had a letter, Alfie. Look."

The boy frowned. Why was his Mum getting so exciting about a letter? Although it was fair to say that he didn't receive a lot of post, it wasn't unheard of for him to occasionally receive a letter. It was usually just junk mail. Nothing that usually caused his Mum to start acting like a little girl who's just caught a glimpse of her favourite pop star.

"A letter?" Alfie repeated, sounding unsure; certain he was missing the reason for his Mum's unbridled excitement.

"That's right, Alfie. A letter," Mrs Jones replied, nodding her head up and down so wildly that for a moment her son was worried it might fall from her shoulders.

Alfie went to take the letter from her hand, but just as he grasped for it, she started bouncing up and down on the spot, inadvertently moving it out of his reach. "It's from a football team, Alfie. I can tell by the badge on the envelope. I had to sign for it and everything, so it must be important. What do you think it could be?"

Upon hearing his Mum's words, the boy instantly froze. Slowly, an expression of pure elation worked its way across Alfie's face. This was it. He was certain of it. Finally, here was the offer... the chance... he had been so desperately waiting for. A trial at Kingsway United!

This time, Alfie snatched the letter from his Mum's hand before she could start bouncing about again. He was just about to rip it open when he noticed something that made him stop.

The elated look on his face was instantly replaced by one of puzzlement.

For while the badge displayed on the envelope did indeed belong to a professional football club, it didn't belong to Kingsway United.

Chapter five

"Well...?" Mrs Jones asked impatiently, imploring her son to share the contents of the envelope with her.

Alfie didn't reply immediately. Instead, he once again ran his eyes over the letter. He wanted to make sure he'd definitely read it correctly the first time.

Sure enough, a closer second reading confirmed that he had indeed understood exactly what was written on the paper.

"Come on, Alfie," his Mum appealed, as he began to read the letter for a third time. "What does it say? Tell me. Please..."

The boy slowly raised his eyes away from the letter and looked at her. A smile started to work its way across his face.

It wasn't by any means a huge, beaming smile, but it was very definitely a smile nonetheless.

"I've been offered a trial for the Norton Town Under 12s Academy," he replied, sounding as though he couldn't quite believe what he was saying.

"Oh my word, Alfie, that's wonderful," his Mum shrieked at the top of her voice. "A trial with an academy! That's what you've been dreaming about for ages, isn't it?"

Without even giving him a chance to reply, Mrs Jones skipped excitedly out of the living room and started shouting up the stairs for Alfie's younger sister, Megan, to come and hear her brother's "wonderfully amazing" news.

"I'm so happy for you, Alfie," Mrs Jones continued as she bounced back into the living room, the volume of her voice slowly starting to return to something like its normal level. "I need to find my phone so I can let your Dad know. Wow. A trial for Norton Town! That's just Gr..." Before she finished her sentence, Mrs Jones turned to face her son. He could see that she suddenly looked more than a little confused.

"I don't think I've ever heard of Norton

Town. They are actually a real football team, aren't they?" she asked.

Neither Alfie's Mum nor Dad had any interest in football. Yet, while they couldn't understand their son's obsession with the sport, and had rarely been to watch any of his games, they were still happy that he had a hobby he was truly passionate about.

That said, there were times, quite a lot of them actually, when Mr and Mrs Jones wished Alfie would spend more time learning and less time thinking about football.

In fairness to Mrs Jones, she couldn't really be blamed for never having heard of Norton Town.

Ever since they had first become a football league team 38 years earlier, Norton Town had never been outside of the bottom division. There was simply no reason why someone who didn't like football or live in Norton would have heard of them.

Alfie laughed at his Mum's confusion and then briefly explained who they were.

However, even once he'd finished his explanation, Mrs Jones still looked unsure.

"I promise they really are an actual

team," Alfie stated, sensing his Mum's uncertainty.

"I'm sure they are," she replied, still sounding a tad baffled. "It's just that... well... I thought you'd be a little, I don't know... happier."

In truth, Alfie did have mixed emotions. While he was certainly pleased – more than pleased, in fact – to have been offered a trial for the Norton Town Academy, there was still a small part of him that felt a tinge of disappointment that the offer hadn't come from Kingsway United. Not only was Alfie a huge United fan who had long dreamt of playing for the team one day, but he already had close friends in the club's academy.

"I am happy," Alfie assured his Mum. "Actually, I'm delighted. It's just that..."

He was just about to explain his thoughts further, when Megan appeared from upstairs.

"What's all the shouting about?" she asked moodily. "I was listening to BoyzHaven's latest song."

"Your brother's been offered a trial with the Norton Town Academy," Mrs Jones answered, unable to stop the pride gushing from her voice.

"Big woo," said a far from impressed

Megan. "Who cares about football? Who are Norton Town anyway? I've never heard of them." Alfie's sister shared their parent's indifference to football.

"Well, I've never heard of BoyzHaven, so who cares about them?" responded Alfie.

Sensing a row brewing, Mrs Jones sensibly stepped-in before things had a chance to escalate out of hand.

"That's enough of that you two. Megan you can go back to your room and listen to your songs. I'm going to give your Dad a ring and get him to pick a pizza up on his way home from work as a treat. And, Alfie, I'm sure you've got some homework to be getting on with."

"Can't we have a Chinese instead?" Megan moaned.

"Do I really have to do my homework?" Alfie grumbled.

"No we can't, Megan. It's Alfie's good news we're celebrating and I know my boy well enough to know he would prefer a pizza," answered Mrs Jones. "And, yes you do, Alfie. Even superstar footballers have to do their homework!"

Alfie seriously doubted the accuracy of his Mum's argument, but after being told that no homework would mean no pizza, celebration or not, he begrudgingly trudged up to his room to get on with some algebra equations that were due in the next day.

By the time Mr Jones arrived home with the pizzas a couple of hours later, Alfie's sense of frustration that the trial offer had not come from Kingsway United had largely subsided.

He'd spent most of the time between going up to his room and coming downstairs for his dinner, texting his friends to let them know about the trial. All of those he had messaged had responded within seconds, stating how fantastic, and well deserved, the news was.

The only close friend he decided against texting was Liam. Figuring that Liam was already annoyed about not being selected for the school's A-Team, he didn't want to risk doing anything that might further annoy him. While Alfie knew that Liam would ultimately be pleased for him, he also realised that his friend would be gutted that he hadn't been offered a trial. 'I'd probably feel exactly the same way,' Alfie had reasoned to himself.

Alfie had also considered phoning Jimmy Grimshaw to let him know.

However, he had ultimately decided against doing so.

Jimmy had been Alfie's first coach when he'd joined the Kingsway Colts' Under 9s. He was now the Head of Youth Development at Kingsway United. It was Jimmy who had offered Alfie a place at the club's Elite Centre, which he now attended every Thursday evening, along with Liam.

While Alfie remained frustrated that he hadn't yet been offered a chance to try out for the Academy, he was still extremely fond of Jimmy. He was also well aware of the fact that the old man had greatly helped to improve him as a player.

As he had contemplated phoning Jimmy, an idea had slowly started to work its way into his head. 'Maybe', Alfie thought to himself as he lazed on his bed, instead of getting on with his homework, 'if I tell him face-to-face, I'll be able to drop enough hints to him that I'd prefer to stay with United... if only they could offer me a trial for the academy.'

He doubted it would work, but figured it was a chance well worth taking.

During dinner, Alfie was greedily tucking into his Hawaiian pizza, when he saw his Mum and Dad share a fleeting peek at each other across the table and then look quickly away the moment they made eye contact.

He studied them for a bit longer, only to notice them go through the same routine three more times.

Watching them more closely, he noticed that both his parents wore anxious expressions on their faces.

"What's going on? What's wrong?" Alfie asked.

"Nothing, Alf. Nothing at all," responded Mr Jones, needlessly rushing his words. "We're just sitting here eating our pizza. There's nothing wrong. Everything's fine. Isn't that right, Mum?"

Mrs Jones almost choked on the slice of pepperoni pizza that she'd been chewing as all eyes around the dining room table settled on her. "No, no, not at all," she replied, once she'd managed to swallow her food sufficiently. "Well... not really wrong, anyway."

"Mum, Dad, Just tell me what's up. This is supposed to be a celebration, yet barely anyone's said a word since we sat down. And I'm not blind. I can see that you're worried about something, just from the way you keep looking at each other."

Mr Jones took a deep breath before

he started to speak. "It's just a couple of things, Alf. Firstly, the date of your trial. We only realised just before dinner that we've already agreed to take Megan and two of her friends to a big netball tournament on the same day and then they're coming here for a sleepover. Their parents are going away that weekend, so we agreed ages ago that we'd look after them. We can't let them down."

"But we'll organise something to make sure you can get to the trial, sweetie, don't worry," added Mrs Jones quickly, noting the look of concern that was rapidly spreading across her son's face.

"Yes," confirmed Mr Jones, "yes, we'll certainly get something sorted out for the date of the trial. But... then... Alf, you have to understand, Norton is around 60 miles away. If you were to make it through the trial and get in to the Academy then the letter says that you'll need to be there two evenings a week. That's a big commitment for us... and you. It would mean I'd have to finish work early to drive you there, and I'm not sure that would always be possible. Then you'd have to find time to do your homework..."

"So, what are you saying?" Alfie asked. His voice was trembling with emotion and he could feel his bottom lip starting to quiver.

Mr and Mrs Jones glanced at each other again; then turned to look at their son. "We'll do everything we can to sort something out, sweetie," his Mum answered, forcing a reassuring smile onto her face. "Let's just see how the trial goes first, hey?"

"That's right," Mr Jones continued. "If you get accepted into the Academy, then we promise that we'll do everything we can to make it work. But... it's just... it's a big commitment. That's all."

"He probably won't even get into the Academy, anyway. He's rubbish" Megan mumbled, frustrated by the lack of attention being paid to her.

Well, if it was attention she wanted, she certainly succeeded in getting it. Both Mr and Mrs Jones turned to their daughter at the same time, making their displeasure with her perfectly clear.

The altercation ended with Megan being sent to her room before she'd finished her pizza. She duly responded by stomping out of the dining room in full tantrum mode, and slamming shut every door she passed on the way to her bedroom.

Yet Alfie remained oblivious to all that

was going on around him. He was too busy worrying that even if he did get accepted into the Norton Town Academy there was a chance he still might not actually be able to join it.

Chapter six

Jasper Johnson seethed as he watched on
enviously from across the playground.

The sight of Alfie being surrounded by
fawning friends was almost unbearable.
Yet, for some reason, he couldn't stop
himself from glaring in their direction.

Discovering that Alfie had been picked
for the main school football team, while
he himself hadn't even been selected
for the B-Team, had been bad enough.
Hearing about Alfie's trial with Norton
Town, though, had taken Jasper's
sourness to another level.

'How has that little muppet managed
to get a trial for a professional football
team?' Jasper wondered furiously to
himself as he kept his eyes resolutely

fixed on his nemesis. 'I'm much better than him. He can't kick a ball anywhere near as far as me!'

The last part of this thought was undeniably true. In fact, very few 11 or 12 year olds could kick a ball as far as Jasper. Some adults couldn't kick a ball as far as Jasper.

Then again, most 11 or 12 year olds were nowhere near the size of Jasper. Actually, come to think of it, some of the teachers at Tideway Secondary School were nowhere near the size of Jasper.

Put simply, in physical terms at least, he was more man than boy.

Jasper's sheer size undoubtedly made him extremely powerful. Very few goalkeepers, if any, would even bother attempting to keep out one of his hardest shots.

They knew that to do so would be to risk a broken limb or the embarrassment of ending up in the back of the net with the ball.

The problem, though, was that very rarely, if ever, did Jasper's shots go anywhere near where he intended them to. At the Year 7 football trials a week earlier, Jasper had insisted on taking a penalty, yanking the ball out of Hayden

Whitlock's hands, despite the protests of all his teammates.

The resulting kick had led to the ball snapping a corner flag rather than bursting the back of the net.

As he continued to scowl in Alfie's direction, the colossal boy considered how brilliant it would be if he could somehow ruin his rival's chance of making it into Norton Town's academy. 'It would be only fair,' Jasper convinced himself. He still blamed Alfie for ruining his own chances of making it at Kingsway United's Academy two years earlier.

Back then, Jasper had surprised everyone by not only being offered a trial at the academy, but actually being selected to join it. Only the very best players in the Kingsway area were invited to join United's Academy – something Jasper most certainly was not.

Initially, Alfie and his friends had believed that Jasper's Dad, Keith, must have been behind his son's selection. However, Alfie, with the aid of Madam Zola, Sammy Reeves and Jimmy Grimshaw, had discovered that Jasper's selection was part of a clever plot designed to ruin Kingsway United's youth system.

It was this revelation that had ultimately led to Jimmy taking over the Academy and Jasper's exclusion from it.

It was something Jasper would never, ever forgive Alfie for.

Yet, try as he might, Jasper couldn't think of anything he could do that would wreck Alfie's upcoming trial. Like football, thinking wasn't one of Jasper's strong points.

He'd considered intentionally injuring Alfie during a kick-about, but quickly dismissed the idea, realising he was unlikely to get the opportunity to do so. Football had long been banned from school grounds during break and lunch times due to the amount of scuffles it caused. What's more, as the Kingsway Colts and Jasper's own North Malling Town team were not in the same league, there was little chance they would play against each other before the date of the trial.

Flummoxed, Jasper eventually managed to tear his eyes away from Alfie and his ever growing band of buddies. "I'll think of something that will wipe that smug smile off your face, muppet, don't you worry about that. You won't stay happy for long," he whispered angrily under his

breath, as he got up and walked to the nearest school door.

"They say that talking to yourself is the first sign of madness, Jasper," remarked Chloe cheerfully. She happened to be strolling past the humongous boy with a bunch of her own friends, just as he'd uttered his curse. Luckily for him, he hadn't whispered loud enough for his words to be heard.

Jasper merely snarled at her by way of response.

"Glad to see you're in as good a mood as ever, Jasper," Chloe chuckled, before turning away from him and rejoining her own group's conversation.

Usually, Jasper wouldn't have been overly interested in listening to a group of other children chatting. Yet the conversation the group were having on this particular day, as he wandered only a few paces behind them, made his ears prick up.

Instantly, a nasty, evil-looking grin replaced the scowl that had been present on his face for most of the morning.

An idea of something he could do to antagonise Alfie slowly started to work its way through his mind.

Okay, so it wouldn't impact in any way on his rival's trial with Norton Town, but it could potentially upset him a good deal.

Such was the bitterness that Jasper felt towards Alfie, any victory he could gain over his much despised rival, would be most satisfactory.

Chapter seven

It was undoubtedly the best goal of the
night so far.

As the ball rolled steadily along the
3G surface towards him, Alfie was
momentarily unsure as to whether or not
he should attempt what he had in mind.
The sight of Jimmy Grimshaw watching
from the sideline convinced him that he
should.

Rather than simply controlling the ball,
Alfie instead flicked it up with his right
foot, before unleashing a powerful volley
with his left. The ball flew through the air
and less than a second later crashed high
into the roof of the net. The goalkeeper
hadn't even had time to move.

"Great goal, Alfie," roared Jimmy,

enthusiastically clapping his hands together.

Pumping his fist with delight, Alfie smiled broadly. Goals like that would be sure to impress Jimmy and the other Kingsway United coaches. 'That won't harm my chances of trying to convince Jimmy to give me a trial for United's academy,' he thought to himself as he jogged back to his position so that the coach could restart the attack versus defence drill.

It was Alfie's third goal of the session, and while he didn't think that Jimmy had seen the other two, the quality of the one he had seen was sure to make up for that.

"You're on fire tonight, Alfie," Liam stated, as his friend hurried past him. "No wonder Norton Town are interested in you."

Alfie wasn't sure whether or not he could detect any bitterness in Liam's voice. Liam had seemed genuinely happy when Alfie had told him about the trial at school earlier that day. Yet not once during the short car journey to that evening's Kingsway United's Elite Centre training session had Liam mentioned the trial.

Neither had his Dad, who took the two

boys to the session most weeks. This made Alfie suspect that Liam hadn't told his father the news. If Mr Walker had known about the trial, then Alfie was certain he would have congratulated him. Maybe Liam wasn't as pleased as he had initially let on.

The coach blew his whistle to restart the drill, making Alfie shake all thoughts of anything but the current session from his mind. Within moments of the attacking team receiving the ball, Alfie pulled left, making an ideal passing angle for the centre midfielder who was in possession. Sure enough, his teammate noticed the run and passed the ball directly to his feet.

This time, Alfie trapped the ball under his left boot, keeping his foot placed firmly on top of it. Quickly raising his head, he noticed that Liam had made a darting run into the area. Rolling the ball out from under his foot so that it moved just a yard or so in front of him, Alfie proceeded to deliver an inch perfect cross, which Liam expertly guided into the goal with his head.

Glancing towards the sideline to make sure Jimmy had seen the cross, Alfie's spirits soared as he witnessed the elderly coach appreciatively nod his head and then give him a double-thumbs up. With that, the old man turned and went to watch one of the other age groups who were training on a different part of the 3G pitch.

'Not bad,' Alfie thought triumphantly to himself as he once again jogged back into position. 'He was only watching for about two minutes and in that time I scored a class goal and set up another. Surely he must be impressed by that!'

The session ended just over half-an-hour later. Alfie listened diligently to the coach's debrief of the various drills they had worked on that evening. He was delighted when the coach singled out his performance as being particularly impressive, and even more thrilled when he noticed that Jimmy was standing nearby, listening.

Once the coach had wrapped-up his talk and sent the players off to find their parents, Alfie was just about to hurry over to Jimmy, when he noticed that Kingsway United's Head of Youth Development was strolling purposely towards him.

"Alfie, I hear congratulations are in order," the old man said, holding out his right hand for the young boy to shake.

Jimmy smiled as he noted the confused expression on the boy's face. "I suppose you're wondering how I already know about the offer from Norton Town, aren't you?" he asked, as he clasped Alfie's outstretched right hand in his own and gave it a firm shake. Alfie nodded.

"Billy and Hayden told me about it last night at the academy session," he explained. "They got your message when they were on their way to training."

Although he hadn't asked anyone to keep the news a secret, there was a part of Alfie that was a bit disappointed to hear that Jimmy already knew about the trial. He had wanted to tell the Colts' former coach himself.

"You must be really excited about it," Jimmy continued, letting go of Alfie's hand.

"Yeah... it's great," Alfie replied, his voice showing little sign of emotion.

Jimmy frowned, an action that only served to further crease his already heavily wrinkled face. "I can't help but sense there's a 'but' coming here."

"It's just, that... well... I always thought that I'd get a trial here. It's my dream to play for Kingsway United one day."

Alfie lifted his face slightly so that it was looking directly at Jimmy's. There was a look of pure pleading on it; as though he was imploring Jimmy to offer him an Kingsway United Academy trial right then and there without actually needing to ask for one.

In turn, Jimmy merely looked sympathetic. "I know it is, Alfie. And you're doing really well here at the Elite Centre. All the coaches say how well you've been performing and you're without doubt one of the most improved players here..."

"So why haven't I been given a trial for the academy yet?" Alfie asked, unable to hold back any longer. "Please Jimmy. Just let me try out! Please?"

With a considerable effort, the old man crouched down, his knees creaking as he lowered himself down to the same height as Alfie. He placed his right hand on Alfie's left shoulder to steady himself. When he spoke, the words came softly. "I'd love to be able to give you what you want, Alfie. It's just that we..." he gestured at himself and the other coaches who were all busy collecting cones, bibs and balls, "... don't think you're quite ready. Not yet anyway."

Immediately, Alfie's face fell. He looked crushed.

Jimmy continued speaking in the same, even tone. "Look, I'm not saying that you'll never be ready. If you keep working hard and improving in the way that you have over the past year, then who knows what could happen over the next few months?" Jimmy took a deep breath and closely studied Alfie's face. He could tell his words weren't soothing the boy at all.

"Trust me on this, Alfie," Jimmy continued, sounding a little sterner now. "The last thing you want is for me to offer you a six-week trial with the Kingsway United Academy when we feel you're not quite ready. You'd probably not last the full six weeks and then how do you think you'd feel? I've seen it happen too many times over the years. Parents put pressure on coaches to get their kids a trial for an academy, and then they get booted off after two weeks because they're not quite good enough. It's a brutal thing for a young child to have to go through and I've seen many children, just like yourself, give up playing football because of it."

Alfie's thoughts flashed briefly to Jasper. His nemesis had barely kicked a ball for a year after his time at the United Academy ended.

Although Jasper had always maintained that his break from football had nothing to do with his disappointment of being let go by United, Jimmy's words made Alfie suspect that it may have affected him more than he had let on.

Slowly, Alfie started to look slightly less downcast. Then he thought of something and the crestfallen expression instantly returned. "Does that mean I won't be good enough for Norton Town, then?"

Jimmy smiled fondly at Alfie. "The situation with Norton Town is completely different," he explained. "All academies are looking for slightly different types of players and Norton have obviously seen you play a few times and decided you have the types of skill they're looking for. You'll still need to work hard at the trial, but just remember to enjoy it."

This made Alfie smile. When Jimmy used to coach the Colts, without fail he would end every single one of his teamtalks with the words 'enjoy it'.

"So, are we good?" Jimmy asked, gently patting the young boy on the shoulder and forcing himself to straighten his knees so he could stand.

Alfie nodded. "We're good," he answered.

Saying goodbye to Alfie, and warmly shaking his hand once more, Jimmy was just about to head off and help the rest of the coaches pack away the remaining bits of kit, when a thought occurred to him.

"You've heard of Monty Capulet, haven't you?" the old man enquired.

Alfie's only response was to look at Jimmy like he was mad. Of course he had heard of Monty Capulet. He was an England international and played for Premier League Westpool Athletic. Everybody had heard of Monty Capulet.

"Well, anyway," Jimmy continued, quickly realising that his question didn't really require an answer from a boy who was as football obsessed as Alfie. "Monty Capulet was turned down numerous times before he made it as a professional footballer. The moral, Alfie, is whatever happens, if you want something you just have to keep working really hard to make it come true." With that, he turned and strolled off to help the other coaches finish packing up.

The boy couldn't help himself from grinning as he watched the old man walk away.

Although the conversation with Jimmy

may not have turned out exactly how he had hoped, if there was one plus side it was that he was now fully determined to focus all his energies on the upcoming trial with Norton Town.

Chapter eight

The day of the first school match arrived.

On their walk to school that morning, the afternoon's game against Longford Hill Secondary School was Alfie, Billy and Hayden's only topic of conversation.

"It's going to be great to play in the same team as you again, Alf," enthused Billy.

"If I even start," replied Alfie. "We don't know what the team will be yet."

"You'll start, without a doubt," Hayden assured him.

"You really think so? Thanks Hayden."

"Definitely." Hayden nodded confidently. "After all, you're the only left footed player that went to the trial who can kick a ball straight."

Alfie wasn't entirely sure whether to take this as a compliment or not. He knew Hayden well enough, though, to realise that he would have meant it as one.

By now, Alfie had largely gotten over the disappointment of being denied a trial at Kingsway United.

He had performed admirably for the Kingsway Colts' a day earlier, scoring twice in a 5-0 drubbing of Melrose Youth. He'd been desperate to do well in that game, knowing that it could be his last Colts' match for a while; possibly even ever.

His trial for Norton Town was to take place on the coming Saturday. According to the letter he had been sent, if he performed well then he would be offered a further six-week trial, during which time he would not be allowed to play for his club side.

If, after this, he was then selected to join the Academy for the rest of the season, it would mean no more playing for the Colts for the foreseeable future.

There was a time, not so long ago, when the thought of not being allowed to play for the Colts would have been extremely troubling for Alfie. He'd once been told by Madam Zola that to become a professional footballer he had to stay with the Kingsway Colts.

However, six months ago the fortune teller had explained to him that he would "have to leave the Colts soon in order to fulfil his destiny," and that he'd "know when the time was right" to leave.

Back then, Alfie had assumed that the right time to leave would be when Kingsway United offered him a trial. He now believed that his future would instead lie with Norton Town.

Thankfully, the issue of getting to the initial trial on Saturday had been solved.

Hayden's Mum had agreed to take him. Hayden had lived in Norton prior to moving to Kingsway a few summers earlier and he had happened to mention to Alfie that he would be visiting family there on the day of the trial.

Alfie had then repeated this news to his parents, who promptly phoned Mrs Whitlock to enquire whether she would possibly be able to drop Alfie to his trial and then bring him home. Fortunately, Hayden's Mum was only too happy to help.

In truth, Alfie was still concerned as to how his parents would manage to get him to Norton each and every week if he did make it through the trial. However, he had resolved to only worry about this if and when he was selected.

His Mum and Dad had promised that they would do everything they could to get him there, and for the time being that was good enough for him.

As the three friends neared the school gates, Alfie suddenly heard a girl call his name. He momentarily cringed, fearing that Daisy Saunders had caught him off guard while he'd been immersed in football chat. Glancing around, and spotting Chloe skipping in his direction, he breathed a subtle sigh of relief.

"Hi guys," she said, as she flung her arms over Alfie and Billy's shoulders. "Looking forward to the game today?"

"Suppose so," Hayden answered, coolly.

"Hadn't really thought much about it," Billy lied.

Chloe smiled, only too aware that the boys were trying to hide their excitement in front of her.

"Do you mind if I borrow Alfie for a moment? I need to talk to him about something."

Billy and Hayden refused to budge. They were intrigued as to why Chloe only wanted to talk to Alfie. Did she have a juicy secret to tell him? Was she going to ask him to be her boyfriend? Billy had long suspected that Chloe had a soft spot for Alfie.

Realising that the other two boys weren't going anywhere, Chloe decided to, quite literally, take matters into her own hands. She grabbed hold of both Alfie's shoulders and shoved him in the opposite direction, marching him quickly away from his mates.

Hayden looked at Billy and shrugged. "Don't worry about it. He'll tell us what she says later anyway," he reasoned.

Once she had propelled him a good distance away from the other two, Chloe stopped marching Alfie and spun him round so that he was facing her.

"Ouch, Chloe that really hurt," moaned Alfie, gently massaging the back of his neck in a bid to try and sooth the pain.

"Sorry," said Chloe, not sounding particularly apologetic. "I was just wondering whether you've had a chance to think about what we were talking about last week?"

Alfie opened his mouth to answer, and then realised that he didn't actually have a clue what Chloe was talking about.

Chloe angrily shook her head and exhaled exasperatedly as Alfie stared vacantly back at her. "About Daisy Saunders," Chloe reminded him, clearly annoyed that Alfie genuinely seemed to have forgotten.

"What about Daisy?" Alfie asked innocently.

Chloe made an angry noise, somewhere between a growl and a grunt, and then took a deep breath to compose herself. "She likes you, Alfie. Remember? I want to know what you're going to do about it?"

"What do you mean 'do about it'?" Alfie sounded panicked. He looked horrified. As white as a ghost!

"Would you like to get to know her better?" Chloe was trying her utmost to remain patient with her friend, but couldn't believe quite how frustrating Alfie could be at times.

"I... I... I don't know," he stuttered. "No... yes... no... maybe. Look, I haven't had any time to think about it. What with the trial, and football training, and the Colts match yesterday, and the game today... I've been really busy."

"So can I give her your number then?" Chloe pressed on, seizing on Alfie's indecisiveness.

"What number?"

Chloe glared angrily at Alfie. She couldn't work out whether he was deliberately trying to irritate her or not.

He wasn't.

"Your mobile number, of course," she replied eventually, speaking slowly, as if she was talking to a first-class idiot.

Alfie looked confused. "So she can text you and maybe arrange meeting up some time," Chloe continued, realising her friend still wasn't quite grasping why Daisy might want his mobile number.

If he was white before, Alfie now looked almost transparent. Chloe had to suppress a giggle. She'd never seen him look so terrified before. "I'll take that as a yes then," she said, before thrusting her hand into his coat pocket and pulling out Alfie's own mobile phone.

"Here, I'll put her number in your phone and then you'll know who it is if she decides to phone you."

"Phone me," Alfie shrieked. "So I'd actually have to speak to her?"

Chloe chuckled and shook her head as she copied Daisy's number from her phone onto Alfie's. "There, all done," she declared, having finished her task and handed his phone back to him. "See you later, Alfie," she said, affectionately rustling his mop of blond curly hair, before striding back in the direction of the school gates.

For a good minute or so, Alfie remained as still as a statue, trying to fathom out what had just happened.

He then glanced down at his phone and scrolled through the list of contacts until he found Daisy's name. He couldn't have told you why, but seeing Daisy's name and mobile number on his phone made him smile.

He then felt a knot tightening in his stomach. It was a feeling he knew well. Nerves. He quite often felt nervous ahead of football matches.

On this occasion, though, Alfie didn't know whether it was that afternoon's match that had caused butterflies to form in his belly, or the fact that Daisy might phone him.

Feeling confused, Alfie strolled back towards the school gates, keeping his eyes fixed firmly on his phone. It would only be later that he would have wished he'd looked up.

If he had have done, he may have noticed that someone else had been listening to his and Chloe's conversation.

Chapter nine

Hayden had been right. When Mr Fowler, the Year 7's football coach, announced the team shortly before kick-off that afternoon, Alfie was delighted to discover that he was starting in left midfield.

Unsurprisingly, Billy and Hayden were also both in the starting 11, as was one of their Kingsway United Academy teammates, Reuben Ryan.

With those three in the team, Alfie couldn't help but feel that their opponents would be in for an incredibly tough match.

So it proved. From the moment the game kicked off it was clear that Longford Hill Secondary School were no match for Tideway.

The match was barely a minute old when Tideway carved out their first goal scoring opportunity. The three United Academy players were all involved.

First Hayden skilfully dribbled past two opponents before playing an exquisite rabona pass to Billy. Perfectly controlling the ball with his first touch, Billy left his marker feeling dizzy as he performed a series of stepovers at such a pace that the defender could hardly see the winger's feet move.

Once Billy was satisfied that he'd completely bamboozled his opponent, he quickly shifted his weight one way and then the other, an action which left the bewildered defender sat on his backside.

He then crossed the ball to Reuben who controlled it using his chest and, without letting it bounce, smashed a powerful volley towards the goal.

The Longford goalkeeper was left with no chance. He hadn't even moved. Unfortunately, the shot was a tad too high and the ball grazed the top of the crossbar instead of bursting the back of the net. It would have been an outstanding goal.

That set the scene for the rest of the match.

Every single time Billy, Hayden or Reuben got the ball, the opposition looked truly terrified. They simply did not have a clue what they could do to stop them.

A couple of the Longford Hill players had tried resorting to foul play in an attempt to disrupt their flow. But even this didn't work. They couldn't get close enough to the three academy players to foul them.

By the half-hour mark, the score was already 4-0, with Reuben and Hayden sharing two goals apiece. Alfie had done okay. He'd set up one of the goals, had played a couple of decent passes and made some well-timed tackles. Like most of his teammates, though, he couldn't help but feel a little in awe of his superstar teammates.

As he watched Reuben jink effortlessly past three opponents for the umpteenth time in the match, feelings of doubts flashed through Alfie's mind.

Were all the players in professional club academies as good as Hayden, Reuben and Billy? If so, was he really at that level? Could he really make it at an academy?

Shaking his head to try and rid himself of all negative thoughts, Alfie decided it was time for him to prove that he could produce skills to rival those of his friends.

Half-time was fast approaching. Realising that with the match already all-but won Mr Fowler would probably look to make substitutions during the break, he figured the quicker he could make a real impact on the game the better.

Moments later, Alfie received the ball out on the left wing. Immediately, Billy, Hayden and Reuben peeled off into space. Without any of them seeming to move too much, all three had instantly created oodles of room for themselves.

The three boys were all screaming Alfie's name, calling for him to pass them the ball.

For the first time in the match, though, he decided to ignore his teammates. This was his time to shine.

Alfie dribbled the ball quickly up the wing, approaching the opposition right back at speed. He knew exactly what he wanted to do. He would wait for the defender to commit to a tackle and then perform an outrageous rainbow flick that would leave his marker as confused as Billy's super speedy stepovers had left his. Alfie had little doubt that it would look awesome.

The perfect rainbow flick involves rolling the ball up the back of one leg with the opposite foot, before flicking the standing foot upwards to propel the ball forward and over the head.

Unfortunately, that's not quite how Alfie's attempt at the trick turned out.

He succeeded only in getting the ball wedged half-way up his standing leg, losing his balance and then falling flat on his face.

Far from the ball looping high over the defender's head, it instead rolled harmlessly to his feet. The sound of laughter, both from opposition players and even some of his own teammates, was utterly humiliating.

Shortly afterwards the referee blew his whistle to signal half-time. The Tideway players all rushed over to Mr Fowler, huge smiles on their faces.

Few of the boys could remember having ever been part of such a dominant team display. The only boy who wasn't smiling was Alfie. He still felt mortified about the dreadful hash he'd made of his attempted rainbow flick.

His misery was compounded moments later when Mr Fowler revealed that Alfie would be one of five boys to be replaced for the second half. Although he knew that it was only fair that the substitutes were given a fair run out, especially with the team already winning 4-0, he'd been desperate to stay on and prove to himself that he could be just as good as Hayden, Billy and Reuben.

"Well played boys. You were all brilliant. None of you have done anything wrong," Mr Fowler assured Alfie and the other substituted boys. "It was always my intention to give all of the subs at least a half. I want to see what everyone has to offer."

Alfie understood, even agreed, with his coach's sentiments. It didn't make him feel any better about being taken off, though.

The second-half continued in much the same vein as the first. The goals continued to fly in for Tideway.

Hayden and Reuben both completed their hat-tricks. Billy scored twice; one a brilliant free-kick which he curled into the top-corner from way outside the area, the other a tap-in from inside the six-yard box.

Annoyingly for Alfie, the boy who replaced him in left midfield, Theo Solanki, also got his name on the scoresheet as Tideway finished the match 9-0 winners.

Billy could see that his friend was feeling a little downcast as they walked back towards the school changing rooms at the end of the match.

"Don't worry about being taken off," he said, patting Alfie encouragingly on the back. "You played really well. Mr Fowler just wanted to give everyone a game, that's all."

"What about that rainbow flick? I made myself look a right wally," Alfie moaned.

Billy was just about to try and convince Alfie that everyone would have forgotten about that by now, when Hayden ran over to join them. "Well that was a bit easy," he stated. "Still, always good to get a hat-trick! Alfie, you're going to have to teach me how to do that trick you tried. I can honestly say I've never seen anyone do..." He halted mid speech, noticing that Billy was glaring at him whilst placing a finger over his lips. "What?" Hayden asked innocently. "It was funny."

Once back in the changing room, Alfie started to make his way over to the bench he had sat on earlier to get changed back into his school clothes, when he noticed something that made him panic.

He was sure he had left his school bag
hanging on a peg above the bench. He'd
left it between Billy and Hayden's, he
knew he had. Yet while he could see that
his two friends' bags were both hanging
there, his wasn't.

Frantically, Alfie rushed over to the
bench, fearing that his bag had been
stolen. It was nowhere to be seen. He was
just about to go and tell Mr Fowler that
it was missing, when Reuben suddenly
appeared holding it.

"I found it on the peg next to mine,"
he said, handing the bag to Alfie and
gesturing to where he had been sitting.

"What was it doing there?" Alfie asked,
as much to himself as to anyone else.
"I'm sure I hung it up here," he added,
pointing to the empty peg between
Hayden and Billy's bags.

"You probably left it in the middle of the
floor and someone picked it up and put
it over there," reasoned Billy. "You know
how untidy you are."

Snatching the bag from Reuben's
hands, Alfie unzipped it and began rifling
through it to check nothing had been
taken. School clothes... maths book...
English book... homework diary... mobile
phone. Everything was there.

Alfie breathed a huge sigh of relief. Billy must have been right. He was sure that he'd hung it up on the peg, but he must have left it on the floor. It was the only logical explanation.

Walking home a little while later, Alfie was feeling a mix of emotions. He was happy that the team had won so easily and, looking back on it, he supposed that he hadn't actually played too badly – ill-advised rainbow flick attempt aside.

He was a little disappointed, though, that his replacement had scored, fearing that Theo would now start the next game ahead of him. He also knew that he'd have to perform much better in his Norton Town trial at the weekend.

Playing alongside Billy, Hayden and Reuben in a real match, rather than just a playground kickabout, had really opened his eyes as to how good you had to be to make it at an academy. It wasn't just about what they could do with a ball – which was a lot – it was also about how intelligent they were off it. They always seemed to be in space; taking up good positions and making it easy for their teammates to pass to them.

He realised he had a lot to learn.

He was still going over and over in his

mind what he could do to improve his game further, when he heard his mobile phone beep.

He plucked the phone out of his jacket pocket, fully expecting it to be a text message from his Mum asking whether he'd be home soon. It was nearly dinner time, after all.

It was indeed a text message. However, it wasn't from his Mum.

Although he wasn't aware of it, a beaming smile had involuntarily plastered itself across his face.

For the message was from none other than Daisy Saunders.

Chapter ten

Alfie doubted his heart had ever thumped so hard in his life. The knot in his stomach had definitely never been tighter.

It was Tuesday afternoon and he was standing in the Kingsway Recreation Ground, beside the rickety old footbridge that spanned the duck pond.

Usually the only reason Alfie ever went to the Kingsway Recreation Ground was to play football. Today was different. Today he was meeting Daisy.

He had been shocked to receive a text message from her the previous afternoon. Although he had agreed to let Chloe give her his number (kind of), he never actually expected Daisy to text him.

Yet she had. And if Alfie was being honest, he was actually quite pleased that she had.

After swapping a few texts, they had agreed to meet by the duck pond.

Alfie had arrived at the pond slightly early. He hadn't meant to. He had meant to arrive late, so as not to appear too keen. Yet he'd become so impatient waiting for their agreed meeting time of four-thirty to arrive, that he'd ended up leaving his house much earlier than he needed to.

He had told his Mum that he was popping out to play football with Billy, Liam and some of the others. He'd then rushed out of the house, hoping that she wouldn't notice he was wearing his smartest jeans, a shirt and his best trainers, instead of his usual scruffy football attire.

As he waited for Daisy to arrive, Alfie was unable to stop himself from jigging about from foot to foot. He could not remember having ever felt so nervous.

When he felt anxious before football games, he at least knew that he would soon settle down once the match was underway. Right now he didn't have a clue what to expect.

What if she didn't like football? Then what would they talk about?

Alfie took his phone out of his pocket and checked the time. 16:26. He was still slightly early.

He was just about to put it back when, as an afterthought, he switched the camera on and turned it to the selfie setting so he could check his hair.

Thanks to the half-a-tub of wax he had plastered on it, his blond curly mop was a little less unruly than usual. Deciding that it now looked as though he'd made a bit too much effort, he ran his hands through his hair in order to mess it up a bit; only to instantly wish he hadn't.

Realising that fussing about his appearance was only serving to increase the number of butterflies swirling about in his already churning stomach, he resolved to put the phone away, taking a quick peek at the time before he did so. 16:28. She was still nowhere to be seen. 'Surely I should be able to see her by now,' he thought to himself.

The minutes passed. There was still no sign of Daisy.

By five 'o clock, the early October air was starting to turn cold. Alfie increased the pace of his jigging, partly through

increased nerves, partly to stay warm.
He knew he'd have to get home for dinner
soon. 'I'll give her five more minutes,' he
mused, craning his neck to see if he could
spot her.

Fifteen minutes later she was still
nowhere to be seen. Momentarily he
considered texting her, then swiftly
decided against doing so. Surely it would
look a bit sad, the fact that he was still
waiting for her forty seven and a half
minutes after they had agreed to meet.

Maybe this was just something girls
did. Agreed to meet you somewhere then
never bothered to show up. Maybe it was
a girl's idea of a joke.

If there was one silver lining it was that he hadn't told anyone else about his plans to meet Daisy; not even Chloe.

He had not wanted any of his friends to tease him. Having to explain to his friends that Daisy hadn't turned up would have been really embarrassing. For that he was thankful, at least.

It was just gone half-past-five when Alfie finally gave up any forlorn hope he had that Daisy would show up. The sky was just starting to darken and he knew it would not be long before his parents texted him, or even phoned, to find out where he was.

Glancing around the park one more time and satisfied that there was no one else nearby, Alfie turned to leave.

It was then the strangest thing happened. Alfie heard footsteps crossing the rickety footbridge behind him, followed by the sound of someone calling his name.

Chapter eleven

He recognised the voice immediately. Not that this in anyway lessened the shock he felt when he turned around.

"W... w... what are you doing here?" he stammered. "I just checked to see if there was anyone else around, and there was no one here. Where did you come from?"

For a moment, Madam Zola looked a little perplexed. "What do you mean where did I come from? I just walked across that bridge there," the fortune teller answered, gesturing towards the rickety old footbridge.

"But you can't have done! I checked. There was no one here," Alfie pressed on, unsatisfied by the old woman's response.

"Where else do you think I would have

come from?" Madam Zola asked, expertly turning her answer into a question. "It's not like I can just appear from thin air, is it?"

Alfie was about to respond that sometimes it felt as though this was exactly what she did, but she continued speaking before he had a chance to say anything. "I've just come to feed the ducks. I do it most evenings. They love a bit of Madam Zola's special homemade bread."

Alfie nodded. That seemed like a fair explanation. Then he noticed something. "But you're not carrying any bread," he remarked, a trace of suspicion in his voice.

The fortune teller glanced down at her empty arms; then looked back at Alfie. There was a look of surprise on her face. "Whoops. I must have forgotten it again." She theatrically slapped her forehead. "You'd be surprised how many times I do that."

Alfie carefully examined the old woman's face, searching for any signs that she might not be telling him the whole truth. He decided that she certainly looked like she was being honest.

"I'll have to go all the way back to get it now," she continued, sounding a little annoyed at her own forgetfulness. "Oh well, it can't be helped I suppose." Madam Zola sighed. Then she looked at Alfie and smiled warmly. Her brown eyes twinkled. "Anyway, it's an unexpected treat to bump into you. What are you doing here?"

"Erm... I've just been playing football with some of my friends," he lied.

Now it was Madam Zola's turn to sound suspicious. "You're wearing very smart clothes for someone who's just been playing football," she said. "Are you sure you're not meeting someone... a girl perhaps?"

Alfie could feel his cheeks burning. "No. I've been playing football. Honest. My football stuff is in the wash so I had to wear this."

"What? All 14 football shirts that you own and all your tracksuit bottoms and shorts are in the wash, are they?" Madam Zola inquisitively raised her right eyebrow and laughed. "You forget, Alfie. I know everything there is to know about you. I know all about Daisy Saunders!"

He was just about to outright deny having ever heard the name Daisy Saunders before, when a thought

91

occurred to him. "Wait a minute. It wasn't you who arranged to meet me here this afternoon, was it?"

Madam Zola looked taken aback. "No, of course it wasn't. Why would you think that?" she asked.

"Because Daisy never showed up," Alfie replied, sounding disappointed. "She arranged to meet me right here at half-past-four, but I've been waiting here for over an hour and there's been no sign of her. I thought... I don't know... maybe it was you texting me, pretending to be her. You know, like you did in that magazine earlier this year."

Around six months previously, Madam Zola had left messages for Alfie in the horoscope pages of one of his sister's magazines. She had called the astrologer 'Jane Folies', as this was a rearranged spelling of Alfie's own name. Unfortunately, he hadn't picked up on the clue until it was too late, and the messages she'd been trying to send him had gone unheeded.

"It's honestly got nothing to do with me this time," she promised. Alfie could tell from her expression, and the way she was speaking, that she was telling the truth. "Anyway, if I had arranged to meet you, I would have been here at four-thirty. Even I wouldn't have known that you'd wait around this long."

The young boy nodded. It was a fair point. "Why do you think she didn't meet me?" he asked. "I really wanted her to." He was surprised by how upset he was at Daisy not showing up.

Madam Zola shrugged. "Who knows, Alfie? I'm sure there will be a good reason, though. There often is."

"Maybe," Alfie sighed. He didn't really think there would be a good reason. He was convinced Daisy was just teasing him; it must be another one of those girl things that boys did not really understand.

"Still," said Madam Zola brightly. "At least you've got the Norton Town trial coming up. I was really pleased when I heard about that. Great news. What a big decision it will be for you. An extremely important one for your future as well."

Mention of the trial instantly perked up Alfie's flagging spirits. "Yeah, I can't wait now. I've got a lot to learn, though. You should have seen how good Hayden, Billy and..." He paused. Something Madam Zola had just said didn't make sense. "What do you mean 'big decision'?"

The fortune teller suddenly looked alarmed. "Is that the time already?" she exclaimed, intently studying her as ever watch-less wrist. "I really must be going otherwise the shops will be shut and I won't be able to buy bread to feed the ducks."

"You said the bread you feed them is homemade," Alfie pointed out, glaring angrily at the old woman.

"It is," agreed Madam Zola. "Homemade from the shop."

Abruptly, the fortune teller turned on her heels to cross back over the rickety old footbridge. "But Madam Zola," Alfie pleaded, "what did you mean?"

"I really must go, Alfie," Madam Zola called over her shoulder, as she hastily strode back across the bridge. "Don't you know that boy behind you?"

Despite himself, Alfie peeked over his shoulder, fully expecting nobody to be there. He was certain the fortune teller was just trying to distract him so she could make her getaway.

Therefore, you can imagine his surprise when he spied the unmistakable shape of Jasper Johnson by one of the park's football pitches. It was apparent that the larger boy was headed in his direction.

Although he was desperate to catch up with Madam Zola and try to find out more – anything, in fact – about what she had meant by 'big decision', he knew he couldn't. Not with Jasper looming so close by. No one was supposed to know about her, after all.

If there was one person that Alfie didn't want to see right at that moment, it was Jasper. Yet he could tell by the way his nemesis was sauntering directly towards him that he had been spotted.

Alfie decided that to run now would make it look like he was either scared of the other boy or had something to hide. He had no choice but to stand and wait for Jasper to walk past him.

"Well, well, well," Jasper called out as he approached. "If it isn't the little muppet, Alfie Jones."

The sneer on Jasper's face was pure evil. Even by his standards. "And who was that?" he asked, pointing in the direction of Madam Zola, who had by now reached the edge of the park and was almost out-of-sight. "Was that the hot date you were supposed to be meeting?" Jasper burst out into a fit of uncontrollable, hysterical laughter.

Much to Alfie's relief, though, he didn't

stop to talk. He just carried on walking, cackling to himself as he went.

Alfie could still hear the sound of Jasper's roaring laughter some 30 seconds later, when he finally turned to leave the park.

For the next hour, Alfie pushed the unpleasant encounter with Jasper far from his mind. His thoughts were dedicated only to his unexpected meeting with Madam Zola.

What was the 'important big decision' he would soon have to make?

He didn't have a clue.

It was while he was sitting at the dinner table, distractedly munching on his third fish finger, that he suddenly recalled something that Jasper had said. He stopped chewing. A frown creased his brow.

How had Jasper known he was supposed to be meeting someone by the bridge?

Chapter twelve

For the remainder of the school week, Alfie did everything within his power to avoid Jasper and Daisy.

He was too embarrassed – and angry – to want to see either of them.

It hadn't taken him long to decide that there was only one possible explanation for what had happened: Daisy and Jasper were obviously friends who had joined forces to play a cruel trick on him.

He was convinced that Daisy never had any intention of showing up at the duck pond. It was all just a 'joke'. A hugely unfunny one, Alfie thought.

Jasper must have been hiding in the park somewhere the whole time, watching him become increasingly anxious as he waited forlornly for the girl to arrive.

The more Alfie thought about how much pleasure Jasper must have gained from what he'd witnessed, the angrier he became. He would have seen him constantly looking at his phone to check the time; seen him regularly playing with his hair – messing it up and then attempting to tidy it again; seen him glancing around every few minutes, desperately searching for a girl who wasn't coming. Worse still, he would have seen the entire conversation with Madam Zola. From a distance, Alfie knew that this would have looked like he'd been accosted by a barmy old lady.

He had waited for Daisy for over an hour! Jasper must have found it hilarious. Alfie felt such a fool!

Jasper and Daisy weren't the only two people who Alfie had determined to steer clear of. He had even taken to avoiding Chloe.

He partly blamed his friend for what had happened. Although he seriously doubted that Chloe would have been directly involved in the cruel trick, it was her who had encouraged Alfie to get to know Daisy better. It was also Chloe who had given the other girl his phone number.

Without her encouragement, Alfie reasoned, he would never have found himself in such a humiliating situation. Chloe was supposed to be one of Daisy's friends. She must have known that Daisy was also friends with Jasper. And Chloe should know better than most that anyone who is friends with Jasper is simply not to be trusted!

It wasn't until Kingsway United Elite Centre training on Thursday evening that Alfie finally forced all thoughts of Daisy Saunders and Jasper Johnson from his mind. Temporarily, at least.

Since Monday evening, he had spent hardly any time thinking about Saturday's trial with Norton Town, and even less thinking about his recent meeting with Madam Zola.

Well, for the time being, attempting to fathom out what the fortune teller had meant about him needing to make a "big decision" would have to wait. Alfie resolved instead to focus solely on football.

By the time the Elite Centre session started, Alfie was in a better mood than he had been in for most of the week.

The second he had clambered into the back of Mr Walker's car that evening, Liam had apologised to Alfie for his moodiness seven days earlier. He admitted to feeling a little jealous of his friend – not only for getting a trial with Norton Town, but also for making it into the school's A-Team. Alfie had assured Liam that it was fine and that he totally understood.

It was true. He did. Had the boot been on the other foot, had it been Liam who had made it into the school team and been offered an academy trial, then Alfie would have been insanely jealous.

Mr Walker also apologised for not congratulating him a week earlier. As Alfie had suspected, Liam hadn't shared the news; he hadn't wanted "everyone going on about it."

Yet for the majority of that evening's journey, the conversation centred only on the upcoming trial. Both Liam and his father were extremely positive about Alfie's chances, with Mr Walker even going so far as to say he could not remember having ever seen anyone improve as quickly as Alfie had in such a short space of time.

Not only did Alfie leave the car feeling

extremely buoyed by the encouraging words of Mr Walker and his son, he was also somewhat relieved to be thinking and talking about football once again.

He was aware that if his trial went according to plan, then this would be his last session at the Elite Centre. If he made the Norton Town Academy then it went without saying that he would no longer be permitted to attend training sessions with Kingsway United.

While there was a part of Alfie that didn't want this to be his last ever session with United, there was a bigger part of him that was desperate for it to be. If it was, then this would mean he had made it into a professional football team's academy! It was something Alfie had dreamed of doing ever since he had pulled on his first pair of football boots at seven years of age.

Right from the start of the session, Alfie was determined to put in as good a display as possible. The better he performed tonight, he figured, the more confident he would feel come the trial on Saturday.

He was also keen to try and be a little bit more intelligent with his movement when he didn't have the ball. Just like

Hayden, Reuben and Billy had been during the school match.

He soon realised it was not quite as easy as it looked.

The coach had decided to run a similar attack versus defence training drill to the one he had a week earlier. Once again, Alfie was positioned out on the left wing. This week, though, he was hardly getting a touch of the ball. Nor was he creating space for his teammates.

Every time he came inside to receive a pass, he found himself either entering an already crowded central midfield area or getting in the way of a better placed attacker. Every time he dropped backwards the ball went forwards. When he bombed up the wing, the ball inevitably went backwards.

After about 15 minutes, Alfie could only remember having touched the ball twice. Both times he had been tackled immediately, having not managed to get away from his marker. It was immensely frustrating.

"Alfie, could you come over here for a moment please," he suddenly heard Jimmy Grimshaw call from the side of the pitch.

As instructed, Alfie swiftly trotted

over to the old man. He had been concentrating so much on the drill that he hadn't actually noticed that Jimmy was even watching.

He assumed that the coach was simply going to wish him luck for his trial. Therefore, he was surprised when he saw that Jimmy had a troubled expression on his face.

"What's going on with you this evening?" Jimmy enquired. "Are you feeling a bit nervous about Saturday?"

The boy shrugged his shoulders. "Not really," he answered, sounding a little perplexed.

"Something's not quite right," Jimmy continued, scratching his head. "I've been watching you for the last ten minutes and you've hardly been in the game at all. In fact, for most of that time you've just been running around like a headless chicken. It's most unlike you."

Alfie explained to Jimmy how he was trying to be a bit cleverer with his off the ball movement. He told the coach all about what he had seen Reuben, Hayden and Billy do during the school match and admitted his fears that unless he could learn to do the same he stood no chance of making it through his trial.

The old man took a moment to digest what the boy was telling him, deliberately nodding his head. "I thought so. The fact is you're trying too hard, Alfie. You've got to remember that Billy, Hayden and Reuben have already had a full season at an academy. In fact, this is Reuben's third season. What you saw them do on Monday were all things they've learned in the past year or two. Your movement is already very good. Think back to last week when you did this exact same drill. You were making space, receiving the ball and scoring and setting up goals. Okay, sometimes you might move more than you have to, but these are things you will be taught if and when you make it through the trial."

Jimmy paused for a few moments to let his words sink in before continuing. "Is this why you attempted that rainbow flick during your school match?" There was the faintest hint of a friendly smirk on the old man's face.

Alfie winced. "Who told you about that?" he asked, although he already knew the answer.

"Hayden did, last night. He showed me it, too. I'd try it myself but I fear I'd never get back up off my bum again."

104

Now it was Alfie's turn to smile. "Yeah, it wasn't my best moment on a football pitch... I just wanted to prove that I could be as good as the other three."

"A-ha," cried Jimmy, clapping his hands together. "That's my point. You were trying too hard again. Not believing in your own abilities."

For a moment, Jimmy considered squatting down to Alfie's height. Then, recalling how much discomfort this had caused him a week earlier, he decided against doing so.

"Look, Alfie," said the old man softly. "As I told you last week, the Norton Town scout – or scouts – have seen something in you that they like. If you really want to stand the best possible chance of making it through the first trial, then it's essential that you play your own game and forget all about trying to copy your friends. Most important of all, though..."

"Enjoy it," Alfie shouted, before Jimmy could finish his sentence.

Jimmy laughed good-humouredly. "Good luck, Alfie," he said, giving the boy an encouraging wink. "I'm sure you'll be fine."

Chapter thirteen

Saturday arrived. Trial day.

Alfie had hardly slept a wink the night before; a mixture of nerves and, especially, excitement, combining to keep him awake. By the time his alarm went off at six-thirty he felt like he had already been awake for hours.

Yet when Hayden and his Mum arrived to pick him up for the long drive to Norton an hour or so later, he didn't feel in the slightest bit tired. He was buzzing; itching for the trial to start.

As he had been instructed to do so in the letter, Alfie was wearing a shirt and tie, smart trousers and freshly polished shoes. He had originally thought that he'd feel a little bit silly wearing these

clothes to football. Instead he felt
something else. He felt professional.

Hayden, meanwhile, looked like he'd
rolled out of bed and grabbed the nearest
clothes he could find; a heavily creased,
seemingly unwashed, Kingsway United
Academy tracksuit.

Twenty minutes into the journey,
barely a word had been spoken by
anyone inside the car. Mrs Whitlock was
listening intently to a boring talk radio
station, while Hayden had fallen asleep
shortly after they had departed and was
currently drooling onto his already tatty
tracksuit top.

This suited Alfie just fine. He was
focussing on the trial ahead and probably
would not have been able to concentrate
on a conversation anyway.

For about the tenth time that morning,
Alfie unzipped his bag to check that he
had packed everything he needed. For
about the tenth time that morning, he
had it confirmed that he had. Everything
was there: his trial letter, football kit,
two bottles of drink, his lunchbox and his
lucky mascot – a teddy bear that Madam
Zola had given to him.

Alfie looked at his boots and shin-pads.
They looked strange. They were clean.

He'd spent much of the previous evening cleaning them; it was the first time he could ever remember having done so.

He wanted to look good for the trial, though. Billy had told him that academies expected their players to look presentable at all times. Glancing quickly at Hayden's scruffy tracksuit, Alfie guessed that he must own more than one.

Hayden was still fast asleep when Mrs Whitlock pulled into the Norton Town training facility some 40 minutes later.

After a considerable amount of prodding and poking from his mother, he stirred briefly to wish his friend good luck, then immediately shut his eyes and fell back to sleep. Alfie thanked Mrs Whitlock and her zonked out son for the lift and got out of the car; Hayden's mum telling him to text her when he was ready to be collected. She then drove off, leaving Alfie standing alone in the car park.

At the opposite end of the car park stood a single building. In truth, it was a quite unremarkable looking building. It reminded Alfie of the leisure centre in Kingsway.

His sights were quickly drawn to the sign placed just above the building's glass-fronted entrance doors. It read:

'Welcome to East Side Park, official training facility of Norton Town FC'.

Just above the sign was Norton Town's logo – a compass with footballs displayed at each of its four points.

For a moment, nerves threatened to overwhelm him and he seriously considered texting Hayden's Mum to ask her to come and get him.

The moment soon passed. Taking some deep breaths to compose himself, he began marching steadily towards the building. He had been told to register there upon arrival.

Not once did he take his eyes off the sign and logo. He did not dare to stop walking or look behind him. To do so, he feared, would be to risk losing his nerve again.

Once inside the building, Alfie gave his name to the young, female receptionist who was sitting behind the long desk in the swish reception area. She ticked his name off on her sheet and then promptly and politely showed him into another, smaller room.

Inside the smaller room were ten or so other boys around Alfie's age. Some were sitting next to adults, many of whom looked even more nervous than the children did. Some, like Alfie, were alone.

Alfie sat down in one of the empty seats and glanced around. Dotted on each of the four walls were numerous painted Norton Town logos, under each of which was a written slogan.

He started to read a few. 'Dare to Win!' 'Nobody who ever gave his best regretted it'. 'A winner never stops trying'. 'Before you can win, you have to believe you are worthy'.

He had read about half of the slogans when a tall, athletic-looking, brown haired young man casually strolled into the room. The man was wearing a black and white Norton Town training top and baggy football shorts.

By now, there were around 30 children, plus some anxious-looking adults crammed into the waiting area. Immediately, everyone fell silent.

In a deep, confident voice, the man introduced himself as Matty Simmons. He was the Head Coach of the Norton Town Under 12s Academy Team and would be overseeing the trial. Alfie could not help but think that Matty couldn't have looked any more different to Jimmy Grimshaw.

Matty explained that in just over five

minutes the boys would be led to the changing rooms where they would be assigned a special training kit for the day. Once changed, they would then be taken down to the training pitches where the trial would take place.

There would be a short break for lunch and then it would be time for more football in the afternoon.

The adults were told that they could wait in the cafe, outside of which there was a balcony where they would be able to view the training pitches from a distance. They would not be permitted pitch-side.

Matty explained that having parents watching up-close, often offering non-too helpful 'advice' to their children, only served to make the boys more apprehensive. This news was met by unhappy murmurs and grunts from nearly all of the grown-ups. Most of the accompanied children, though, seemed to perk up a bit upon hearing this.

Ten minutes later, Alfie was standing in a changing room, staring at his reflection in a full-length mirror.

He could hardly believe what he was seeing. He was kitted out in an actual football kit belonging to a real-life

professional football team. It was a
dream-come true.

Suddenly, from out of nowhere, nerves
threatened to consume him. He'd never
felt like this before. Not even when he
had been waiting to meet Daisy by the
duck pond a few days earlier.

There were no butterflies in his
stomach. No feelings of nausea. Instead
he felt drained of all energy. His legs
seemed to have turned to jelly. It was
taking all the effort he could muster just
to be able to stay on his feet.

He stumbled over to the nearest bench,
trying his best to make it appear like
he wasn't struggling to walk. He could

feel beads of sweat breaking out on his forehead, as though he were burning up. Alfie started to panic. What if he had caught a fever at the worst possible time?

Thankfully, one of the adults in the room seemed to notice Alfie's discomfort and rushed over to him.

"It's Alfie Jones, isn't it!" the man stated rather than asked. He held out a hand for Alfie to shake.

With a great a deal of strain, Alfie managed to raise his arm just enough to be able to give the man a pathetically limp handshake.

"I don't feel too good," Alfie moaned.

The man laughed. "I'm sure you'll be fine, lad. It's just nerves. Most of you will be feeling the same way. Take a look."

The man gave a sweep of an arm, inviting Alfie to look around the changing room.

Alfie slowly swivelled his head left and then right. Straight away he saw that many of the other boys appeared to look as bad as he felt.

Some were sat hunched over on benches, eyes fixed firmly on the floor. Others looked so pale that they seemed to have been drained of all colour. Above the changing room's noise, Alfie was sure he could even hear a couple of boys vomiting in the toilets. At least he hoped they were in the toilets!

"We see things like this all the time, lad" the man continued. "It's good when we see children getting nervous. It shows us that they care."

Briefly, Alfie wondered if Hayden and Billy had felt nervous before their trials with Kingsway United. He could not imagine either boy ever feeling anxious ahead of playing football. He made a mental note to ask each of them at a later date.

"Anyway, lad, if you play like I've seen you play before, then you'll have nothing to worry about."

"Y... y... you've seen me play before?" Alfie stuttered.

"Aye. Indeed I have, lad," the man answered, nodding his head. "A few times, in fact. The first time was just over six months ago. I wasn't even supposed to be working but I happened to pass a game going on in the Kingsway Rec so decided to stop and watch for a while. You had a stormer that day, lad. Scored a blinder. Took one touch and then curled the ball right in the top corner. Lovely stuff."

Instantly, Alfie knew what game the man was talking about.

It was the final game of the previous season; he had scored both goals in a 2-1 victory that had led to the Kingsway Colts avoiding relegation. The goal the man had described was probably the best Alfie had ever scored.

"I've seen you play a couple of times this season too, lad," the man added. "You've impressed me both times. I love the desire you have for the game; I've not seen many players who work as hard as you do. Anyway, good luck. The name's Noel Forint by the way, lad."

With that, the scout walked swiftly off in the direction of one of the other pale-looking boys. "It's Giorgio Rossi, isn't it," Alfie heard Noel say as he approached the other boy.

Gradually, Alfie could feel his energy returning.

Hearing Noel's praise had helped to relax him.

He was still nervous, sure. But he was now feeling the type of nerves he was used to prior to a game. The butterflies, increased heart rate... he knew once he got on the pitch he would be alright.

Which was lucky, because seconds later

Matty Simmons entered the changing room.

It was time for the trial to begin.

Chapter fourteen

"So how did it go?" asked a rather more awake Hayden, as Alfie slid wearily onto the backseat beside him.

"Okay," Alfie replied. He was too exhausted to expand any further.

The truth, though, was that the trial had gone rather better than just 'okay'.

Much of the trial had consisted of match-based scenarios, which were Alfie's absolute favourite type of training session. Over the course of the day, Alfie had scored quite a few goals and set-up even more.

Noel Forint had been particularly enthusiastic in his praise for Alfie.

Yes, Alfie believed the trial had gone very well indeed.

117

Now all he could do was wait.

Towards the end of the trial, the trialists had been gathered back together in the small room in which they had started the day. They were then informed that letters would be sent out during the week, letting them know whether or not they would be invited back for a further six-week try out.

Matty had gone to great lengths to warn the boys that there were only limited places available and that not everyone would be invited back.

He had urged those who were unsuccessful on this occasion not to be too disappointed and to keep working hard. They were all good players, he had assured them.

Clipping in his seat belt so that Mrs Whitlock could start the drive home, Alfie knew that there would be a few sleepless nights in store as he waited for the letter to arrive.

"I remember the morning of my trial at United," Hayden said, clearly not in the mood to let Alfie doze in the same way that he himself had on the way there. "I was so nervous that morning that I felt sick. It was horrible. I'd never felt like that before."

Alfie nodded. He understood exactly how his friend would have felt.

"Billy was sick," Hayden continued, barely pausing for breath. "It was horrible. There was sweetcorn and bits of chopped up carrots everywhere."

"Hayden, that's disgusting," Mrs Whitlock admonished.

"Just telling the truth," Hayden answered, matter of factly.

Arriving home an hour or so later, Alfie's parents were both keen to discover how the trial had gone.

He gave them a rather more in-depth description than he had given Hayden and Mrs Whitlock.

In fact, he spent more than 45 minutes giving them a complete step-by-step breakdown of the day. He described in great detail what the facility was like, enthused about how great the coaches were and how friendly everyone seemed to be. He explained to them what he thought he had done well during the trial and what he did not think he had done quite so well.

The truth was that, having no real knowledge of football, Mr and Mrs Jones understood very little of what Alfie was saying. Yet this fact did not bother them in the slightest. Neither of them could remember the last time they had heard Alfie so excited or could recall the last time he had spoken to them for such a lengthy period. It was simply wonderful to see him so enthusiastic.

Once he had eventually finished giving his detailed account of the day, Alfie was just about to ask his Mum and Dad whether they had yet given any thought as to how they would get him to Norton every week if he was offered the six-week trial, when the house telephone rang.

Mrs Jones answered it, spoke briefly, and then held the phone out for Alfie. "It's for you," she said.

Alfie wandered over to take the phone from his Mum, wondering who could be calling him.

At first he expected it to be one of his friends, ringing to find out how the trial had gone. He then decided it was far more likely to be someone like Jimmy. His friends would almost certainly have rang – or more likely text – him on his mobile.

However, as it turned out, the caller was neither Jimmy nor any of his school friends.

Chapter fifteen

"Hello Alfie, lad. It's Noel Forint," the man on the other end of the phone said.

Alfie was so surprised to hear the Norton Town scout's voice that he dropped the phone. After a brief fumble, he managed to catch it just before it hit the floor. He quickly lifted it back to his ear.

His hands were shaking so much that he had to press the phone tightly against his face to stop himself from dropping it again.

"Are you still there, lad?" Noel asked, sounding confused.

"I... I... I'm here," Alfie replied, trying desperately to regain his composure. Mr and Mrs Jones weren't quite sure what to make of their son's sudden strange behaviour.

"I've got some good news for you, lad," Noel continued. "Matty was very impressed by what he saw of you today. I've been telling him for months about what a good little player you are, and I'm not sure he really believed all that I was saying. Until today, that is..."

Alfie's heart skipped a beat and then began to race. He pressed the phone even harder against his face as it once again threatened to slip from his increasingly shaky grasp.

"Anyway, we don't normally do this over the phone, lad, but we were both so impressed with your performance today that we've decided to make an exception. Norton Town would be happy... no, delighted... to offer you a six-week trial."

For a moment Alfie said nothing. He was speechless.

Then, without warning, he let out an almighty squeal of delight – one that made both his baffled looking parents jump with fright. He started dancing around the living room, roaring triumphantly. He could not remember having ever felt so happy.

It took Alfie a good couple of minutes to

calm down enough to be able to continue his conversation with Noel. He had been so busy dancing and waving the phone about like a pom-pom, he'd temporarily forgotten about the man on the other end of the phone.

Ceasing his celebrations, and placing the phone back against his ear, Alfie could hear Noel laughing. "I take it you're pleased then, lad?"

"It's... it's the best news ever!" the boy exclaimed. "I... I... don't know what to say. Just... thank you so much!"

Noel chuckled again. "That's alright, lad. You'll get a letter in the week confirming what I've just told you. That will explain what nights training will be held and give details of the commitment we expect from you during the six weeks."

Subtly, the tone of Noel's voice altered ever so slightly, becoming just a touch more serious. "Just remember, lad, it's during this six-week trial that the hard work really starts. Only the very best players with the right attitude get picked for the Academy. Don't think you've made it just yet."

Alfie assured the scout that he would not let him down.

"I know you won't, lad," Noel said, his

tone brightening again. "Good luck. See you soon."

Alfie thanked the scout again and said his goodbyes.

Hanging up the phone, the boy turned to face his parents. Both wore beaming smiles on their faces.

"I take it that was good news," Mr Jones stated – or rather understated.

"It was the best news ever! Norton Town have offered me a six week trial! I'm going to have a real chance of getting into a professional team's academy."

For the second time in the space of half-an-hour, Alfie was just about to enquire as to how his parents would get him to Norton each week, when he was again interrupted from doing so. This time by the living room door being flung open.

"What's going on in here?" Megan moodily demanded to know. "Me and my friends are trying to watch all the BoyzHaven videos on the computer and all we can hear is Alfie shrieking."

Alfie had forgotten that his sister had some of her friends staying the night. Normally this would have annoyed him, but this evening he was so happy that he doubted whether anything could upset him.

"He's just excited, pudding," Mrs Jones explained. "He's just been offered a six-week trial with Norton Town."

Megan looked distinctly unimpressed. "So? We're trying to watch BoyzHaven videos. I think that's rather more important, don't you?" A mischievous look suddenly spread across Megan's face. "Anyway, it's only a trial. There's no way he'll actually get selected. He's rubbish."

She looked expectantly at her brother, gleefully relishing the angry reaction her taunt was sure to get.

"If you say so, Moggy," Alfie replied, smiling sweetly at his sister. "Go and watch your videos with your little friends. I heard on the radio today that the lead singer is leaving to pursue a solo career," he added, untruthfully.

Megan glared at her brother. "No he isn't," she snapped, although she sounded doubtful. She couldn't believe that he had reacted so calmly to her deliberate provocation.

Angrily spinning on her heels, Megan marched out the door and slammed it shut behind her. Barely a second passed before the door re-opened. "And don't call me Moggy!" she screamed, before slamming it again.

"I wish you two would get along at least some of the time," Mrs Jones sighed frustratedly.

"She started it," Alfie remarked, obviously pleased to have ruined his sibling's plan whilst managing to wind her up at the same time. "Anyway," he continued, before taking a deep breath. "I was just wondering whether... I mean, how... have you? ... I don't know... thought about how you're going to get me to Norton each and every week?"

Mr and Mrs Jones glanced at each other and then turned to face Alfie. They both wore doubtful expressions. Alfie started to worry. He was certain his greatest fear was just about to come true. That he was just about to have the chance of making his dream come true shattered before it had even started.

"Look, Alfie," Mr Jones began in his most soothing tone. Alfie bristled, fearing what his Dad was about to say next. "Norton is a very long way away. Having to get there in rush hour traffic one, maybe even two, evenings a week is a huge commitment. A massive one."

Alfie closed his eyes. He didn't like the direction his father's answer seemed to be heading in and he wanted to stem the flow of tears that he knew would follow.

"But..." continued Mrs Jones. She was speaking even more softly than her husband had been. "...we also know how much this means to you. I've never seen anyone react as excitedly as you did when you were speaking to that man on the phone. Not even Megan when we got her those BoyzHaven concert tickets for her birthday. It's not going to be easy, but we'll do everything we can to get you there each week. Hopefully your grandparents will be able to help out a bit, too."

Alfie slowly opened one eye, then the other. Tears were indeed rolling steadily down his cheeks. But they were tears of joy rather than those of sadness. Within seconds they were flowing like a waterfall. "Yesss," he shouted, punching the air with one hand while wiping the tears off his face with the other.

He ran over to his parents and, to their immense surprise, flung his arms around both of them at the same time, squeezing them together in an almighty bear hug. "You're the best Mum and Dad EVER!" he proudly proclaimed.

Sitting in his bedroom a little while later, Alfie reflected on what he felt had easily been the best day of his life. It was a day he was sure he would never forget.

Even the noise of his sister and her friends loudly giggling and squealing in the room next door as he tried to settle down for some much needed sleep could not put a dent in his good spirits.

It was as he lay awake in his bed, listening to Megan drone on and on about how great BoyzHaven were, that a thought suddenly popped into his head, seemingly from nowhere.

He'd had such a busy few days, what with the Daisy and Jasper incident and then the trial, that he had barely paid any thought to his latest meeting with Madam Zola.

It felt like months had passed since he had last seen her. Not days. Yet laying awake that night, the words the fortune teller had spoken to him by the duck pond earlier that week came flooding back into his mind.

"At least you've got the Norton Town trial coming up," she had said. *"I was really pleased when I heard about that. Great news. What a big decision it will be for you. An extremely important one for your future as well."*

So far as Alfie could see, there was no

decision to be made. He had been offered a trial with Norton Town and he would accept it. Where was the big, important, decision there? For once Madam Zola must have been wrong.

Pushing all thoughts of Madam Zola from his mind, Alfie pulled his pillow over his head to try and block out the sounds coming from Megan's bedroom. He soon fell into a deep sleep.

However, if there was one thing Alfie should have known by now, it was that Madam Zola was never, ever wrong.

Chapter sixteen

For once, Alfie could not wait to get to school on Monday morning. He was eager to tell all the friends he hadn't yet told about his six-week trial offer.

Yet this wasn't the only reason he had for leaving his house extra early that morning. The squad for the Year 7 football team's second match, scheduled for Thursday afternoon, was also due to be announced. He was keen to discover whether he had kept his place in the squad – even though he was fairly confident that he would have done.

Arriving at school long before the first bell sounded, Alfie headed directly to the PE Department to see whether the squad list had been pinned to the notice board.

He had just entered the corridor in which the changing rooms were located, when he saw Liam walking purposely in his direction. From the beaming smile on his friend's face it was clear that Alfie wasn't the only one with good news to share that morning.

"Hey, Alfie, guess what?" Liam yelled excitedly.

"No idea," Alfie replied, shrugging his shoulders.

"I'm in the A-Team for this week's match!"

Alfie struggled to hide his surprise. Having won 9-0 in their first game, he had been fairly certain that the squad would have stayed the same, "Erm... wow... that's great. Congratulations."

Liam noticed Alfie's reaction and smiled. "Don't worry. You're still in the squad, superstar. They're not going to drop their Academy hotshots now, are they?" He gave Alfie a playful punch on the arm to show that no malice was intended.

Liam had been one of the first people Alfie had texted his news to a day earlier. The only close friend he hadn't messaged was Chloe. He was still angry with her regarding the whole Daisy situation.

"The truth is," Liam continued, "I'm

quite surprised. I didn't think I'd have any hope of being selected after your win last week. But I thought I'd check all the same. Mr Fowler has obviously come to his senses," he added with a smile.

"Cool. I'm really pleased for you, Liam. I was quite shocked when you weren't picked to begin with, to be honest."

"So was I," Liam responded, as modest as ever.

"I'm going to take a look at the squad anyway," Alfie continued. "See if I can work out who you've replaced. Coming?"

"Nah," Liam replied. "I'm going to find Billy and Hayden and tell them I'm going to be their teammate again. The goal machine is back!"

Alfie laughed as he watched his friend jog down the corridor, air kicking an invisible football and then raising an arm in mock celebration as he went.

He turned to go and look at the squad list himself, but had barely taken more than a step when he noticed something that made him freeze.

Standing at the far end of the corridor, carefully studying the notice board outside the girl's changing room, was Daisy Saunders.

Alfie felt like a rabbit trapped in a

car's headlights. He was fairly certain that Daisy had not yet seen him and he wanted nothing more than to get out of the corridor before she did. But for some reason his legs wouldn't move. It was as though his feet had been super-glued to the floor.

To his horror, Daisy suddenly stopped looking at the board and turned round. She was staring right at him.

"Hi Alfie," she called, smiling sweetly. She had just started walking towards him when finally his legs began to work. Instantly he spun around and bolted in the opposite direction.

As he turned the corner at the end of the corridor he heard Daisy calling after him. "Alfie, wait, I need to talk to you," she shouted. There was no chance he was going to let that happen, though. Not after the way she and Jasper had humiliated him. He would never trust her ever again.

Within seconds, he had caught up with Liam who was still searching for Billy and Hayden.

"Where are you going in such a hurry?" Liam asked as Alfie raced past him.

"I thought I saw Billy heading this way," Alfie shouted back over his shoulder. He hadn't, of course, but there was no way he was going to tell Liam that he was running away from a girl.

"Really?" Liam said, scratching his head. "Wait for me then." With that, he took off after Alfie, pursuing him for a good 30 seconds before Alfie finally slowed his run to a walk, allowing his friend to catch up with him.

Figuring he was by now a good distance away from Daisy, Alfie stopped walking and leant against the nearest wall. He was breathing heavily.

Liam did likewise. He, too, was puffing and panting. "I thought you said you saw Billy?" he said breathlessly, using one of his hands to wipe sweat from his brow.

"I guess I must have been wrong," Alfie replied. "Come on, let's get moving," he urged. He did not want to stay in one spot too long in case Daisy caught up with him. "The first bell is due to ring soon."

Liam sighed. "Give me a moment. I'm not used to running that quickly so early in the morning," he puffed.

"We need to go now, Liam. Let's go!" Without waiting for a response from his friend, Alfie moved away from the wall and began marching in the direction of his tutor group's classroom.

Liam glanced suspiciously at his friend and then begrudgingly started to follow him down the corridor. "Are you sure you're alright, Alfie?"

"I'm fine. I told you, I just thought I saw Billy and wanted to catch up with him before school starts. I won't see him until break time otherwise."

There was something about the mixture of irritation and defensiveness in Alfie's tone that made Liam suspect his friend was not being entirely truthful. The quick peeks that Alfie kept taking over his shoulder were also a little odd. However, not being of an overly inquisitive nature, Liam decided to let the matter drop.

They had neared Alfie's classroom, when Liam suddenly remembered something. "Oh, I forget to tell you. I saw Chloe earlier, when I was on my way to the PE Department."

Alfie looked at Liam, but didn't say anything.

"Are you two still friends?"

"Yeah, suppose," Alfie answered sullenly. "Why'd you ask?"

"Well, when I mentioned your six-week trial to her, she didn't seem to know anything about it. Then she seemed really upset that you hadn't texted her to tell her yourself."

"Erm... I guess I just forgot," Alfie said sheepishly. He suddenly felt a pang of guilt about the way he had been treating her. Chloe was one of his oldest and closest friends. Maybe he was being a bit harsh, blaming her for what had happened with Daisy.

Arriving at his classroom door just as the first bell sounded moments later, Alfie said goodbye to Liam and went to sit at his desk.

By the end of that morning's geography lesson he had resolved to go and find Chloe as soon as he could and apologise for having avoided her for the past week.

If there was one thing he was sure of it was that he did not want Daisy and Jasper's nasty trick to spoil his friendship with Chloe.

Chapter seventeen

By the end of the school day, Alfie had
been unsuccessful in his mission to speak
to Chloe.

Although he had seen her around school
on a couple of occasions, both times she
had been with a group of friends that
included Daisy.

He was now waiting for Hayden, Billy
and Liam by the school gates, whilst
keeping half an eye out for his best – in
fact his only – female friend. He soon
spotted her. Once again, though, she was
with Daisy.

Worried that the other girl would see
him, Alfie tucked himself behind a nearby
rubbish bin in order to hide until they
had passed by.

He was still crouching down behind the bin when Billy and Hayden arrived a few seconds later. "What are you doing, Alf?" asked a rather flummoxed looking Billy.

"Erm... just looking for something that I've dropped," Alfie fibbed.

"Oh, what is it?" Hayden asked. "I'm really good at looking for things. Well, as long as I don't have to move anything to find them, I am."

"Erm... erm... it's... oh look, there's Liam," Alfie stated, pointing at their friend in a bid to deflect attention away from himself.

"Oh yeah. How long do you think it will be before he mentions something about being selected for the school team?" Billy asked.

"About 30 seconds," Hayden guessed.

"Nah, it'll be less than that," Billy declared confidently. "What do you think, Alf?"

"Found it," said Alfie, quickly plunging a small twig into his trouser pocket before Billy and Hayden could see what 'it' actually was. "What do I think of what?"

There was no time to explain. Liam had already joined them by the bin. "Hello teammates. The school team's newest star striker is here!"

Billy looked pointedly at Hayden. "Told you," he said.

"You win," Hayden agreed.

"Told you what? Win what?" Liam asked. "By the way, why are you all standing by a bin?"

"Don't worry about it," Alfie answered hurriedly. "Let's go."

Alfie only lived a 15-minute walk away from school. However, such was the relaxed pace at which the four boys dawdled as they talked about their days, that it always took him closer to 45 minutes to arrive home.

Finally arriving at the end of the road in which he lived, Alfie said farewell to his three friends and then pulled his mobile phone from his jacket pocket.

He contemplated sending Chloe a text, but didn't really know what to say. By the time he reached his front door, there was still a blank space on the screen where the message was supposed to go.

He put the phone into his trouser pocket, fished out his keys and opened the front door. 'I'll just speak to her tomorrow,' he mused. 'It will probably be better to speak to her face-to-face anyway.'

Alfie removed his jacket and went to hang it on one of the hooks by the front door. There were four hooks; one each for his parents, and then one for him and one for Megan.

To his astonishment, there was already something hanging on his. A long, green, thick woollen knitted jumper. There was only one person that Alfie knew who wore jumpers like that.

He moved swiftly into the front room. Sure enough, sitting in an arm chair, nursing a warm cup of tea, and deep in conversation with Mrs Jones, was Jimmy Grimshaw.

"Hello, sweetie," Mrs Jones said as she swivelled round to face her son. "Jimmy's come to see you," she added, rather unnecessarily.

"I can see that, Mum. My eyes do work, you know. Hi Jimmy."

"Hi Alfie," Jimmy replied, raising a hand in welcome.

"Okay, there's no need to be smart," said Mrs Jones, sounding a little put out. "Anyway, I'll leave you two to it. Jimmy's already been here for half-an-hour. I don't know why it takes you so long to walk home from school, Alfie, really I don't. Would you like another cup of tea, Jimmy?"

The old man smiled and shook his head. Mrs Jones left the room.

It was obvious to see that Alfie was extremely puzzled to see Jimmy sitting in his front room drinking tea on a Monday afternoon.

"So then, Alfie, I suppose you're wondering why I'm here?" the old man asked as the boy sat down on a stool opposite him.

"You could say that," Alfie replied, nodding his head.

"Well, I've got some news, Alfie. Some news I thought you'd be interested to hear."

Chapter eighteen

Alfie leant forward on his stool, staring intently into Jimmy's face.

He had absolutely no idea what the old man's news could be. However, he knew that if Jimmy had taken the trouble to come to his house just to tell him, then it must be important.

In turn, Jimmy relaxed back into his comfy chair, and stretched his long legs out in front of him. He then took a sip of tea, and placed the mug onto a mat on the table beside him.

"Now, what I'm just about to tell you," the old man began, "is something I probably shouldn't really be speaking about. But as you'll see, there's a reason why I thought I should let you know now, rather than at a later date."

The boy leaned closer to Jimmy. His blue eyes opened a little wider. Every ounce of attention he possessed was at that moment focussed solely on the man sitting opposite him.

A band of dancing gorillas could have come jiving into the front room and he wouldn't have even noticed. Put simply, he was utterly intrigued.

"Last week, Kingsway United received a grant from the Football Association to expand the academy," Jimmy started to explain. "What this means is that from next season the number of boys being invited to train at the academy for the under 13s to the under 15s age groups will increase from 16 to 20."

By now, Alfie was leaning so far forward on his stool that it was a wonder he had not fallen off.

Jimmy picked up his mug of tea, took another sip, replaced it on the mat, and then continued speaking. "Over the weekend I asked all my staff to start putting together a list of players that they think could potentially make up one of these four extra places in each age group. I got the lists back from them this morning. Your name was on every single

143

one that was handed to me by the coaches of your age group!"

We've all seen those cartoons where a character's eyes pop out of their sockets and their mouths open so wide that their jaw, quite literally, hits the floor. That's exactly how Alfie looked as Jimmy finished speaking and gulped down what remained of his tea.

"You mean," Alfie exclaimed, barely able to contain his excitement, "that I'll definitely have a trial for the Kingsway United Academy next season!"

Jimmy frowned and scratched his chin with his right hand. After taking a few moments to consider his response, he said: "I wouldn't say 'definitely'. But there's certainly a fairly good chance. Say, maybe, 70 per cent."

Alfie leapt from his stool, sending it crashing to the floor. "Whoo-hoo," he yelled loudly. He was just about to thank Jimmy for the unbelievably good news when he noticed the expression on the old man's face. He didn't look pleased. He looked troubled.

"Please, Alfie, don't get too excited, there's a but coming. Sit back down and hear me out."

As requested, Alfie picked the stool up

off the floor, stood it up and sat down. The expression on his face now mirrored that on Jimmy's.

"As I said, there's no guarantee that you'll definitely be offered a trial. I can't, and won't, promise that you will be. What I can say, though, with absolute certainty, is that we won't invite anyone who is already connected to another academy for a trial. It's a Kingsway United policy not to poach children from other professional clubs."

Alfie immediately understood what Jimmy was trying to tell him. Should he be offered a place in Norton Town's Academy following his six-week trial, then if he were to accept, he would have no chance of being offered a trial for Kingsway United.

"I'm sorry, Alfie," Jimmy sighed sympathetically, noticing the pained expression on the boy's face. "I wasn't sure whether to tell you, but knowing how desperate you are to play for United's Academy, I felt it was only fair to let you know. I'll leave you to think about things for the time being. You always know where I am if you want to talk things over."

Alfie, though, was now barely listening

145

to what the old man was saying. He was too busy thinking back to what Madam Zola had told him during their previous meeting by the duck pond.

He now knew what the important big decision she had told him he would soon have to make was.

Chapter nineteen

Unsurprisingly, Alfie found sleep almost impossible to come by that night.

He could not stop all the different scenarios from whirring round and round in his mind. The more he thought about his options, the more his head spun.

On one hand he actually felt quite fortunate. If he attended the six-week trial with Norton Town, and didn't get selected, then there was a decent chance that he would be offered a trial with Kingsway United a few months later.

This gave him two chances to get into an academy. He knew that not too many boys got opportunities like this.

However, what if he was selected? Obviously this would be amazing.

Getting into a professional football team's academy was something he had dreamed about for years.

But – there always seemed to be a but lately – this would then mean that there was no chance of him getting a trial for United at a later date. They were the team he supported. The team he had long dreamed of playing for. What's more, he also already knew three players who attended the Kingsway Academy – Billy, Hayden and Reuben. At Norton he didn't know anyone.

Of course, he could always turn down the Norton offer (if he got one) or even decide not to attend the trial.

But – see, another but – what if he was then not offered a trial with Kingsway United? Jimmy had told him that the offer wasn't definite. Around a 70 per cent chance he'd said.

This still left a 30 per cent chance that he would not be offered one. Could he really risk turning down an opportunity with Norton Town on a mere possibility?

Then there was the knowledge that even if he did get offered a trial with Kingsway United, there was still no guarantee that he would be selected to join the academy.

It was all just too confusing.

On top of all this, he could not shake Madam Zola's words from his mind. She had described the 'big decision' he'd have to make as being 'extremely important for his future'.

This led Alfie to believe that if he chose the wrong option it could seriously harm his chances of one day becoming a professional footballer.

The fact that he was unable to tell anyone else about Madam Zola did not help matters.

His parents had both advised Alfie to attend the trial with Norton Town, even though it would be easier for them if he got into the Kingsway United Academy.

"It's better to go for the offer that's there, rather than for one that isn't," Mr Jones had explained, quite reasonably.

Neither Mr or Mrs Jones could understand why their son didn't seem to feel the same way. Especially given the sheer delight he had displayed upon being offered the trial with Norton Town only two days earlier.

Yet what if this was the wrong decision? What if he was supposed to turn down Norton Town in favour of Kingsway United? What if by joining Norton's

Academy he was somehow putting his dream of becoming a professional footballer at risk?

He had no idea what to do for the best.

The dilemma was still plaguing his mind as he left his house to walk to school on Tuesday morning.

Unlike the previous day, when he had departed earlier than usual to get to school, this morning he purposely left about 10 minutes later than he normally did.

Although Alfie, Liam, Billy and Hayden never arranged to walk to school together – they would always be late if they did this – more often than not they would catch up with each other somewhere on route. Today, though, Alfie didn't want to meet up with his friends.

If he was alone then he figured there would be more chance of Madam Zola making one of her sporadic appearances.

If he was with other people he knew there would be no chance of this happening. She only ever met the boy when he was by himself.

He was desperate for another hint from Madam Zola regarding the decision he faced. Therefore, by leaving his house later than normal, he had reasoned there would be less chance of bumping into any of his friends and more chance of encountering the fortune teller.

He was wrong.

He had barely taken a step out of his front garden and onto the pavement when he heard someone call him.

"Oi, Alfie. I want to talk to you."

He recognised the voice instantly. Craning his neck and peering down the street, he saw Chloe leaning against a lamppost. It was obvious that she had been waiting for him to emerge from his house.

Initially, Alfie sighed deeply, annoyed to have had his plan to walk to school alone ruined already. Then, remembering that he was eager to make amends with the girl, he shook the disappointment away and hurried over to her. The confirmation letter had not arrived from Norton Town yet, so there was still time for Madam Zola to appear before he would have to accept – or refuse – their offer.

"Hi Chl–," Alfie began to say. Chloe, though, was not in the mood to let Alfie talk.

"What exactly have I done to upset you?" she bellowed. Her green eyes flashed with anger. She'd roared so loudly that a few people in the nearby houses had peaked out of their windows to see what all the commotion was about.

"I've always thought that you were one of my best friends," she said a little quieter, aware that she was making a scene. There was still no hiding the anger in her voice. "But over the past week I've barely seen you."

Alfie attempted to speak again, raising both his hands as he did so in a gesture to try and calm Chloe. He had never seen her so angry. "I can exp–."

"At first I didn't think anything of it," the girl raged on. She was clearly determined to get what she wanted to say off her chest before she would allow Alfie a chance to talk. "Maybe he's just really busy, I thought to myself. It's not like we speak every day anyway. I'm sure he'll text me to let me know how his trial went."

"But Chl–." Alfie once again tried to enter the conversation. Again he was unsuccessful.

"Yet Saturday I didn't hear from you. Sunday I didn't hear from you. I figured the trial must have gone really badly or something and that you were too gutted to want to talk. That's fine, I thought to myself. I'll see him at school and we'll catch up then."

Chloe took a deep breath and paused for a moment. Believing she had finished her rant, Alfie went to speak. But before he could even get a word out, Chloe continued her verbal onslaught.

"Then, on Monday morning, what do I discover? Not only had your trial not gone badly, it actually went well. Very well in fact. A six-week trial! Amazing news! The sort you'd want to share with everyone. But do you tell me? Oh no! I have to find out from Liam – who you'd texted along with all your other friends a day earlier. Well, all your friends accept me. Still I was prepared to give you the benefit of the doubt. Maybe you wanted to tell me specially? I don't really know why I thought this. Just did. Then worst of all..."

The girl took another deep breath. Alfie could see that tears were starting to form in the corners of her eyes. She was shaking with emotion. He felt terribly guilty.

"... Worst of all, I saw you yesterday. After school. I know you saw me, too. Don't try to deny it. You were staring straight at me. And what did you do? Did you come and speak to me? Come and tell me how brilliantly your trial had gone? No. You went and hid behind a bin. So I ask you again, Alfie. What exactly have I done to upset you?"

Alfie waited a moment before answering. Partly because he was trying to figure out how to respond; partly because he wasn't entirely sure whether or not it was his turn to speak.

When Chloe said nothing further, Alfie cleared his throat. "I'm really sorry, Chloe," he stated meekly.

"You're sorry?" Chloe repeated quietly. There was a sinister hint of menace in her tone. "Is that all you've got to say for yourself?"

"No... no... look, let me try to explain." Now it was Alfie's turn to take a deep breath. "I know it was wrong to avoid you this past week. And I know I should have texted you to tell you about the trial. But I promise I wasn't avoiding you yesterday!"

"So you weren't hiding behind the bin when I saw you?" Chloe countered.

"No... erm... I mean... yes... I guess," Alfie stuttered. "But not from you," he added quickly. "I was actually looking for you. I wanted to speak to you... but... but

Daisy was with you."

"Oh, Alfie grow up," Chloe snapped. "Just because I told you she liked you there's no need to act like such a big baby."

With that Chloe turned and stormed off in the direction of the school. Alfie rushed after her.

"I'm not being a big baby," he pleaded, as he pulled up alongside her. "It's just after what happened at the duck pond last week... I don't want to see her again. It was really humiliating."

This made Chloe quit her steady march. She gazed quizzically at Alfie, who had likewise stopped walking. "What do you mean, 'after what happened at the duck pond last week?'"

Alfie explained almost everything that had happened a week earlier. He told Chloe about arranging to meet Daisy by the duck pond. About having waited there for ages (although he only admitted to having waited for around 30 minutes rather than for over an hour). About Jasper's sudden arrival and the fact the other boy had hinted that he knew Alfie was meant to be meeting a 'date'. He even told Chloe how he had wrongly blamed her to some extent for what had happened. The only thing he omitted to tell her was about the meeting with Madam Zola.

Upon finishing his tale, Chloe looked completely baffled. "None of that makes sense," she pondered. "Daisy told me only yesterday that she hadn't been able to text you yet. She accidentally dropped her phone down the toilet – don't ask me how – last Monday evening and hasn't got a new one yet. I guess this explains why you ran away from her in the corridor by the changing rooms yesterday. Don't look at me so surprised. She told me all about it."

Alfie scratched his head. "But it was last Monday evening that she started texting me. After the school match."

"Give me your phone for a minute," Chloe demanded, rather than asked.

Alfie did as instructed. Chloe tapped the screen a few times, then took her own phone out of her school bag and did likewise.

Satisfied, she held the two phones out so that Alfie could see their screens. "The number on your phone doesn't belong to Daisy," she explained. "It's completely different, see. There's no way that's the number I gave you."

"Then whose number is that and how did it get on my phone?" Alfie enquired.

"Just give me a moment," Chloe answered. She copied the number on Alfie's phone onto her own and pressed the call button. Whoever had messaged Alfie may already have his number, but Chloe was fairly certain they wouldn't have hers.

It went straight to voicemail.

Unfortunately, the voicemail greeting was the standard one issued by the service provider, rather than a personalised one from the phone's owner.

"Hmmm, we'll have to try it again later," she said disappointedly. "Oh dear," she exclaimed, noticing the clock displayed in the corner of the phone's screen. We need to get going. We're going to be late for school."

Chapter twenty

Chloe was right. They were late for
school. Very late.

So late, in fact, that both children were
instantly handed a 30-minute after-school
detention for that day. It was the first
detention that either Alfie or Chloe had
received since starting at Tideway.

Fortunately, the teacher in charge of the
detention, Miss Plant, seemed to be as
fed up about being there as the children
were.

"I don't mind what you do for the next
half-hour," she told the eight children
sitting in the classroom, "just so long as
you don't make any noise and disturb me.
I've got some marking to do and if I really
have to be in here with you lot then I may

as well make the most of the time."

Alfie opened his bag and briefly considered making a start on the biology homework he had been handed that afternoon. However, noticing that last week's edition of *Kick Off* magazine was crumpled up at the bottom of his bag, he instead pulled that out, smoothed the paper as best he could, and began reading.

Five minutes later he gave up and stuffed the magazine back into his bag. Reading about football had only succeeded in making his mind wander back to the dilemma regarding what he should do about the Norton Town trial. In fairness, such thoughts had rarely been far from his mind all day.

He'd considered asking his friends for advice, but ultimately decided against doing so.

For one, he wasn't entirely sure whether he was allowed to share the news that Jimmy had given him regarding the imminent expansion of the Kingsway United Academy.

For another, he knew that without knowing the whole story, his friends were almost certain to give him the same advice that his parents had. Namely, do the Norton trial and see what happens.

The only way to explain his reluctance to accept the Norton trial would be to tell his friends everything – including the part about Madam Zola.

Aside from the fortune teller's warning not to tell anyone else about her, Alfie had another reason for wanting to keep her existence a secret. He was well aware that if he started telling his friends that a fortune teller called Madam Zola was helping him to fulfil his dream of one day becoming a professional footballer, they would probably think he was an utter loony.

Alfie took a pen out of his pencil case and grabbed a piece of scrap paper off a nearby table. He drew a line down the centre of the paper, splitting the page into two columns. His intention was to write the plus points of accepting the Norton Town trial and a possible place in their academy on one side, and the advantages of waiting for a possible Kingsway United offer on the other.

Although he had been over the pros and cons of each option many times in his mind, he figured that having it all written down might somehow help him to make a decision.

He was just about to put pen to paper when Miss Plant suddenly stood up at the front of the classroom. "Right, I need a coffee," she declared. "A teacher cannot be expected to mark all this drivel... I mean work... without lots of caffeine inside her. I'll be back in two minutes. Stay quiet, I'll be listening for any noise."

With that she strode quickly out of the classroom. Alfie watched her go and then turned his concentration back to the piece of paper in front of him.

He was just about to start writing when he was again distracted from doing so. This time by something striking the top of his head. Alfie turned around to see what was going on just in time for a second crumpled page from a magazine to hit him squarely in the face.

The assailant was Chloe who was sitting at the desk located directly behind him. "Alfie, give me your phone," she whispered urgently, just loud enough for him to hear.

"Why?" Alfie whispered back.

"I want to try that number again. I accidentally deleted it off my phone earlier. Quickly, otherwise Miss Plant will be back."

Alfie shrugged his shoulders and yanked

the phone from his coat pocket. He was about to hand it to his friend when he paused. "Don't get it confiscated."

"I won't, just give it here. Quickly!" Chloe said, rather than whispered, impatiently.

Chloe swiped the screen, tapped it a few times, found the number she was looking for and once again copied it into her own phone. She dialled. Alfie eagerly studied Chloe's face. He wondered what she would do when the person on the other end of the phone answered. It quickly became clear, though, that her plan had once again been thwarted.

"Still on voicemail," she confirmed, handing the phone back to Alfie whilst pulling a face that made it look as though she'd just sucked on a lemon.

Alfie swivelled back round to face his own desk. For the third time he picked up his pen, determined to make a start on his list. For the third time he was distracted from doing so. Something on one of the crumpled magazine pages that Chloe had thrown at him had caught his eye. He picked it up and began to smooth the page as best he could.

At that moment, Miss Plant re-entered the classroom. She looked distraught.

"The kettle's broken," she stated, in a tone which suggested she had just been given some tragic news. "I can't make myself a coffee!" She glanced up at the clock on the wall. "Well, you've been here for about 15 minutes, that's close enough to half-an-hour for me. You're free to go home." With that she charged back out the classroom, no doubt bound for the nearest coffee shop.

All the children whooped with delight, grabbed their bags, coats and any other belongings and practically sprinted to the door.

Well, all accept Alfie.

He sat motionless, completely engrossed in reading the magazine page Chloe had chucked at him.

"Are you coming, Alfie?" Chloe asked, wandering back into the room having realised he had not followed her out.

"Erm... give me a minute," he replied, without removing his eyes from the page.

Chloe sighed frustratedly. "I'll wait for you outside. Maybe I'll try that number again while I wait." Alfie flashed his friend a thumbs up to indicate that he had heard her. Again, though, he did not take his eyes from the page in front of him.

A minute or so later, he stopped looking at the page and raised his head. A gigantic smile had spread across his face. He carefully folded the piece of paper he had been reading, not wanting to crease it any further, and placed it in his bag.

Standing up and strolling outside, he saw that Chloe was waiting for him on a nearby bench. She looked as pleased with herself as Alfie did.

"What are you so happy about?" she asked, noting Alfie's joyful expression.

"Because I now know what I have to do," he answered, nodding his head with a degree of certainty. "What about you?"

Chloe laughed triumphantly. "I know who texted you."

Chapter twenty one

The page that Chloe had thrown at him had been severely crumpled.

Yet as he had settled down to try and write his list, Alfie just so happened to glance at the paper missile. His eyes were instantly drawn to two words.

They were: 'Jane Folies'.

This was the very name that Madam Zola had once used in a bid to attract his attention. Rearrange the letters of Jane Folies and you get Alfie Jones. It was one of the many frustratingly cryptic puzzles that the fortune teller seemingly enjoyed setting him.

Upon uncrumpling the paper, Alfie had been unsurprised to find himself staring down at a horoscopes page.

Without a moment's hesitation he searched for his own starsign, Libra, and began reading:

Decisions, decisions. It often feels like life is full of decisions. Should I do this? Should I do that? What happens if I do this? What will happen if I do that? Sometimes, though, the only person who can make the right decision is you. Go with your gut instinct and do what you think is right. Just remember, the path to your dream may not always be the one you would have expected to take.

He had reread the passage over and over again. There was something familiar about the last sentence. It took him a few reads to recall that Madam Zola had spoken almost the exact same words to him a few weeks earlier inside Sammy Reeves' shop.

No sooner had Alfie remembered this, did the clouds of confusion that had been floating through his mind for much of the past 24 hours immediately clear.

He had always thought that if and when he was selected to join an academy, it would be Kingsway United's.

He had never thought about the

possibility of being offered a trial with another club. Not ever.

Suddenly he was certain what Madam Zola had meant by suggesting that the path to his dream may not necessarily be the one he had expected to take. His future lay with Norton Town. Not Kingsway United.

As he had sat alone in the classroom, Alfie thought about how well his trial with Norton Town had gone. How welcome he'd been made to feel; especially by Noel Forint who really seemed to rate him highly as a player.

Deep down he knew that the only reason he might possibly get offered a trial with Kingsway United was because the academy was expanding. If it wasn't for that fact, then they probably would not have been interested in him.

Jimmy had almost said as much when Alfie had begged him for a trial shortly after he had received the initial offer from Norton.

He'd walked out of the classroom in high spirits. Not only was he once again eagerly looking forward to his six-week trial, he was also supremely confident that he would ultimately be selected.

That the confirmation letter from

Norton Town was waiting for him when he arrived home from school later that afternoon, was taken by Alfie as a further sign that Norton Town was where he was meant to be if he was to fulfil his destiny.

The only puzzle now remaining to Alfie was the identity of the person who had pretended to be Daisy.

He had begged Chloe to share her discovery with him as they walked home from school following their detention, but his friend had remained resolutely tight lipped. "Meet me after school tomorrow and, hopefully, all will be revealed," was all she'd said.

It was now Wednesday afternoon. As arranged, Alfie met Chloe by the school gates after school. Chloe had been walking in a group of girls which included Daisy.

This time, though, Alfie didn't hide behind the bin when he saw her. In fact he even managed to return Daisy's friendly wave with an awkward one of his own.

The group of girls had all 'ahhed' when they saw this. Alfie's cheeks turned a bright shade of pink. He suddenly wished he had hidden behind the bin again.

They had now been walking for

about 15 minutes. Instead of the usual leisurely pace at which Alfie was used to strolling home from school, today he was practically jogging to keep up with Chloe. Wherever it was she was leading him, she wanted to get there fast.

During their journey, Alfie continually questioned Chloe about where they were going and why. Still, though, the girl refused to answer any of his questions. "Stop talking and keep walking," she ordered. "We're almost there now."

About five minutes later they arrived at the entrance to the Kingsway Recreation Ground. "In here," she said, turning into the park.

Alfie looked perplexed. "What are we doing here?" he asked.

"I'm meeting someone," Chloe responded. "Now keep quiet and get behind that big tree."

With that Chloe shoved her friend none too gently in the direction of the tree she was talking about. She then raised a finger to her lips, urging Alfie to keep quiet.

Alfie sighed grumpily and rolled his eyes but did as he was told.

"Keep your eyes peeled that way," Chloe hissed under her breath. She pointed to indicate which way he should look.

"But I don't know what I'm looking for," Alfie whispered in response.

"You will when you see it. Now shhh!"

Alfie was getting fed up with Chloe's strange behaviour. It reminded him of being with Madam Zola. Still, utterly intrigued by whatever it was that Chloe wanted him to see, he once again did as instructed.

He had been staring in the direction that Chloe had been pointing for about five minutes, when he saw something that horrified him. "Oh no," he murmured.

"What is it?" Chloe asked. Even though she was whispering, Alfie felt he could detect a hint of glee in her question.

"Jasper's here," he sighed. "I just saw him by the children's playground. I think he may be coming this way. I can't let him see me here with you behind this tree. He'll spread stupid rumours around school."

Chloe grinned and started bouncing excitedly up and down on the spot. "What's he doing?"

Alfie watched with horror as Jasper continued walking steadily in their direction.

Then, much to his relief, the large boy turned left. "It looks like... I think... yes... he is definitely... he's heading for the duck pond. He's now standing there. I think he's waiting for someone."

"He is." Chloe smirked.

"How do you know?" Alfie asked, bemused.

"Because he's waiting for me!"

From the way Alfie looked at Chloe you would have thought her skin had turned green and she'd spouted a second head from a shoulder. "What," Alfie shrieked. "Why do you want to meet Jasper?"

"Keep your voice down," Chloe muttered angrily. "You really are a bit of a doughnut at times aren't you, Alfie? It was him all along."

"What was him all along?" Alfie whined. Why couldn't anything ever be simple?

Not for the first time in the past few weeks, Chloe glared at Alfie like he was a complete imbecile. "The person who messaged you was Jasper. When I rang that number yesterday it was him that answered. I hung up immediately, of course."

"But Daisy's name came up on my phone," Alfie mused. "How is that possible?"

171

"He must have got hold of your phone and edited his number under her name. You must have been careless and left it lying about."

Alfie was just about to refute this point. He always had his phone on him. It was either in his inside jacket pocket or, if he wasn't wearing his jacket, in a trouser pocket. There was no way Jasper could have gotten hold of it. The only time he didn't have his phone was...

"I've got it," Alfie exclaimed, clicking his fingers. Chloe urgently hushed him. "It was in my bag when I played for the school team last week. After the match my bag had been moved. It was hanging on Reuben's peg instead of mine. He must have got into the changing room while we were playing and done it then."

Chloe nodded. "That must be it. Someone probably came into the changing room while he was doing it and he panicked and hung the bag back up in the wrong place. Although this is Jasper. He might have just genuinely forgotten where he'd taken the bag from.

So that was it. Mystery solved.

Almost.

"So why did you arrange to meet Jasper?" Alfie asked.

Chloe smiled. "Let's just call it payback," she said. "Come on, let's go home."

***

Jasper Johnson had been shocked when Chloe had approached him during break time that morning.

Aside from his own friends, of which there were only two, hardly anybody else ever bothered to go and speak to him. Least of all girls.

He was even more surprised when Chloe told him that she'd had a crush on him for quite a while and wanted to meet him after school.

Initially Jasper was suspicious of the offer and said he would think about it.

Having thought about it during the maths lesson between break time and lunch he quickly became less suspicious.

Was it really that hard to believe that a girl had a crush on him? After all, not only was he one of the school's best footballers, he was probably the best looking boy in Year 7 as well. He was a catch. Why would Chloe not fancy him! She'd be mad not to.

At lunchtime, Jasper went looking for Chloe. He found her chatting with

173

her group of giggly friends and decided against going over to speak to her.

Talking to the girl by herself was one thing, doing it in front of all her friends, quite another.

Fortunately, Chloe had spotted him lurking nearby and gone over to speak to him. They arranged to meet that afternoon at the duck pond in Kingsway Recreation Ground.

Jasper had raced home from school that night, jumped in the shower, pulled on the best clothes he could find, and smothered his face with half a bottle of his Dad's best aftershave. He then rushed out of the house and headed quickly to the duck pond.

Which is where he was now. He glanced down at his watch. 16:05. She was already five minutes late. 'That's alright,' Jasper thought to himself. Even he knew that girls were useless when it came to time keeping.

She would be here soon. He knew she would.